T0137624

Princess Yvonne

Edward H' Wolf

Order this book online at www.trafford.com
or email orders@trafford.com

Most Trafford titles are also available at major online book retailers.

Printed in the United States of America.

ISBN: 978-1-4269-5056-8 (sc)
ISBN: 978-1-4269-5057-5 (e)

Trafford rev. 12/16/2010

 www.trafford.com

North America & international
toll-free: 1 888 232 4444 (USA & Canada)
phone: 250 383 6864 • fax: 812 355 4082

Declaration

$\mathcal{M}$y declaration statement in discernment to the facts set forth in motion that: WARNING: This novel is fiction. It contains adult language; violence; adult sexual content and situations not intended for those under 21 years of age; adult supervision is strongly advised and recommended.

The characters came from another realm; that of imagination and used for the sole purpose of fiction not those of living breathing people and their namesake that I foreclose my actual knowledge to you John P and Jenny Q Public this fact by the virtue of things that go bump in the night inside fiction subjected to content in the midst of insanity and, not to be confused with reality.

None of these events ever took place; and the imaginary dead cannot and will not speak out in protest because their characters fit the eras ever so slightly that I have placed them in here to draw your mind's eye into an unreal world where you may experience visions or nightmares, but don't fret, they are not real and will not harm you. Younger readers may need to seek an adult to guide them because the young just simply can not and will not understand or make a distinction between that which it real and not real; I also state further this deals with witchcraft of which I do not believe in, and do not practice and neither should any of you the patrons who partake of this with their minds to view and read the content set forth here-in this fiction novel.

to display sections for any promotional public display as deemed necessary with me the author and the foresaid mentioned others and with their discretion.

It is further so stated that critics may reproduce only short sections for review, Publishing firms, the media, and authors, and for the purposes that shall be deemed necessary for the retailing and promotion of this novel, and or any book signings to be established at such a time deemed necessary by the publisher, editor, or by this author. The final decision to this matter is my personal preference and final choice to make in the end.

Dedication

$\mathcal{D}$edicated to my very best friend the beautiful - sweet Vera…whom I treasure deeply; my sister Letha, and my 5 kids, Eddie III, Michael, Kevin, Christopher, and Jennifer… without them I'd be lost and all alone in this world.

To all of the great authors Poe, King, Spielberg, Sterling, Twain, and so many more who have given me so much inspiration that it haunts me to know their spirits still flourishes deep inside of my wondering existence that lay with-in this delicate and unknown world of the all-seeing mind's eye.

My spirit is filled with sincere and humble gratitude for all here who helped me in my novel achievement and whom encouraged me throughout my writing career.

I thank you all, very sincerely.

Edward H' Wolf

Introduction

My name is Princess Yvonne of the castle Davenport. Being a lady and a Princess Royal foremost is not amusingly an easy task in combination to one another, especially in this realm of intrigue with mythical mystery and magic; furthermore, especially if you have talents such as I have. I am an absolute divine creature of a different species and my character is most becoming if I may take the liberty to say so myself.

I hail from another time where life has its many difficulties and a time where life is both giving and taking. One must be cautious to embark on such practices as the Angleland Craftism beliefs such as Ich and my people the Fairies have, as well as some humans especially when young.

My parents the High Prince Zelstar of the Goddess' Gideon, who be my father, and my dear mum, the Mother of all Goddess' Shauna, may the good spirits of our Angleland Craftism beliefs rest their weary souls if they still have them in the world of the beyond, where ever that realm might be; could it be in the kingdom of God, or could it be in the pits of hell with the devil?

It was they… my parents who controlled this land and the peoples that dwell here-in; it was they who kept the true evil forces from spreading unkindly spells through-out this land, and it was they who brought up myself and my step-sister Stella the now evil princess of the Black Dragon of, in and for the eastern partition that is desolate and full of wickedness in my country. It is she who now practice the evil parts of our Angleland Craftism beliefs.

Once I was lying naked under the stars near my humble but quaint dwelling near the equinox of my wonderful Castle Davenport when I was sold out, yes I said, I was a sold out fairy witch of a Goddess Stella, my step-sister trod to the tune of pure evil in her Craftism practices and brought many wicked spells to our household shortly before our parents passed to the great beyond of spirits. Our mother who had the upper hand in the household as well as most of it on the outside walls of Castle Davenport caught my step-sister Stella casting one of her evil spells late one night and was furious with her over such evil in her presence and the presence of Mother Earth and Father Sky who brought us to this land, nurtured us in the proper rituals of spell casting for good, and not evil like Stella was dabbling in on a daily basis.

Mother pulled her by her long black hair, threw her to the floor and then destroyed all the evil expertise tools of the great skill along with the meddlesome potions, and then she took her Shadow Casting Spell's book bound from the leather of a diseased Wart Hog and told her to get out of the house of Davenport; never return unless she repented from her evil ways. The spell book was locked away in the tower at the east end of the castle away from my presence and also to be hidden away from thieves and the likes of other witches in practice with evil minds; so that they too would not use it for their own foul purposes. Stella went off that night to the North- East and never returned to this day, and that was two long years ago when I was in my early stags of puberty at the tender age of ten years and six months old.

My practice was of the Angleland Craftism nature as well as being my religion so to speak, if you believe in such things or not, that is the way it was for many beautiful fairies and human women with poor young souls such as mine in a time of marvels beyond your wildest nightmares and the utmost of solemn dreams that is in the mind's eye are of a simple blue sky nature filled with much radiance that I use my craft for good and with the intensions of making our land safe once again just like it use to be when my parents were alive, and not for the pure evil of seeing just how far one can really take this practice of spell casting and other evil doings.

My psyche of consciousness allows me to create ambers so overwrought with fire and power that the struggle for survival in everyday life amongst the living as well as the dead brings me to a new place in time; a place where only the most powerful will triumph their life long excursions.

Table of Contents

Chapter 1
Plotting the Quest for Blood

The stream that flows by my castle had beautiful flowers growing in abundance along its banks until that fateful day in early spring time in the year 1489 when an epidemic of the Bubonic plague in mass proportions broke out in the village of Alexandria near the Castle of Davenport here on our Holy Mother Earth. Castle Davenport was hailed by my parents the High Prince Zelstar of the God of Gideon and my beautiful mother the Mother of all Goddess' Shauna Goddess of Clay Ribs who hails to be the most powerful and most beautiful witch amongst all of the Angleland Craftism beliefs and cult witches in our land.

I, Princess Yvonne am the only one of my generation who can thank her famous father for the lips that have become her blotch. I was born in 1475 to the pillow-lipped High Prince Zelstar of the Gods in Gideon, and my dear mum, the Mother of all Goddess' Shauna in a time when Witches, Warlocks, Dragons, Ogres and the likes ruled and roamed the still untamed lands of the world of the weird, insane, beastly, the destructive as well as the tame and domesticated mild mannered who were always frolicking amongst black magical spells, famine, and the dreaded disease the Bubonic Plague or better known as the Black Plague or Black Death of the late 13th century of 1489 month and year of the dragon in merry 'ol Alexandria Angeland whereby lie the Castle Davenport; mine home.

I the little Princess Royal Yvonne have been raised mostly by my dear mother and even my father when he wasn't out and about slaying other people or bad things. I found myself on my own at the ripe old age of 14 when both of my wonderful parents passed away to an untimely demisemiquaver from the Black Death.

After this adolescent' parent's deaths while I was still a teenaged woman, I had a choice to either be a vagrant and roam the countryside, or stay in Castle Davenport to do fantasy exploration so that I would come to grow of age into adulthood; a task that most would dread; but for myself; well, it was a thing of beauty and ease from the pure Mother Nature and wise old father time that I'd been blessed with from birth.

From time to time I did a fairies amount of theft during some of my nomadic peripatetic roving as a practiced Witch as well as a Princess, living in places such as Middlesex, Thames, and now back in the place of my birth… Alexandria where somehow I'd found my own way back to claim the Castle Davenport to become the rightful ruler of merry old Angeland as I should have been from the time of my parents' death's.

I am but a fledgling Fairy Princess making some historical acting productions known throughout the land as rightful heir to the throne of Angeland and have became a powerful ġeong hēah (young high) Princess Royal of witchcraft in the more widely fantasy realm of which I dwelt amongst my peers, both ġeong and old in a similar way.

My first taste of recognition came to me in the form of a handsome man called Sir William John Thames the Guardian of Welsh one day during one of my pilfering escapades to survive and devise a plan to end the terror of the demon Dragon and my one time evil step-sister Stella while still doing the best I could to be the Princess and ruler over all the land of Angeland and its surrounding territories and continents, but not many recognized me as being of Royalty… to them I was just a pain in the ass child and not much more than that.

Little was it known to my lȳtel ġeong (little young) mind that Sir William and I would be married in a very brief time?

After appearing in a number of mediocre places with the mighty and handsome man Sir William John Thames the Guardian of Welsh in my view… I Princess Yvonne finally began to make a big hit amongst my people; and began to give off winning performances throughout my home town and surrounding territories with speech after powerful speech telling people that they would soon be free from the demisemiquaver demis (dame) Stella who caused the black death she had created from a witchery spell, and took on a demonic black dragon as her protégé of further destruction, and had began to gain respect from the locals causing me to become famous as well as wide spread amongst all the worlds nomadic tribes; indeed I, Yvonne was a true ruler and much needed Princess and world leader that would ultimately bring peace through-out the vastness of even the real and natural world as well as to my Fairy's fantasy realm that I now dwell in.

The plague is a highly toxic infectious epidemic disease fatal to almost all who come in contact with a poor soul that is a carrier of the dreaded ailment from those pests, those awful lȳtel bugs that transmit a bacterium when they have bitten an gullible host, giving way to a high fever, chills, and the formation of buboes under the arm or in the groin areas of humans and beastly creations alike, spreading their dark dismal and foul odors about the land as if they had been placed there by the very flames of hell themselves. This foulness must be eliminated quickly before they all perished in their own filth amongst the worst of thieves and the like which dwell in this beautiful kingdom of the mid age Europe and its 13th century iniquity, wickedness, and impieties of sin, lustful ways and the likes in a time of tragic and unwanted foul smelling and irrevocably decayed diseased blackened death of a devil's pestilence associated with his evil and demonic ways.

The Devil's hands are always busy creating and molding his hideous moans with lots of unreasonable and needless miseries that inflict bodies and make them rot before our very eyes; the rotting bones of the dead lay along path after path and against building after building, letting the wild dogs and other wondering despicable varmint chew at their flesh for the necessary nourishment that sustain their own lives, but with one draw-back, they end up with sickness and vomit the decay back upon the earth to be spread still further by and to many more such vermin and victim alike. It is they, the destructive animals and insects that harm our people, our livestock, and stink up our property with the foul disease.

We have so tried to make our crops safe from all the animal and human waste that is left behind, but the stench cannot be cleaned just by washing them off with lye. Pests such as rats, maggots, fleas, and cockroaches are difficult to control, extremely unpleasant, and highly undesirable to contend with at any point; be it day or be it night; we just have to clean things up the best that we can and continue to walk through our daily lives as delicately as possible in the milky white midst of this dreaded and unwanted disease… the Black Plague of death.

My role would soon be coupled with playing life by heart; and, would be followed with many adventures in the shortness to the quest that I and my newly found companion Sir William Swordspoint of the village

Alexandria and a few others whom would soon embark upon an insane quest to end evil within and outside of the kingdom; and, my to the plight amongst some who want to claim my castle in the sky along with this lȳtel chicks mind's eye of daydream, vision, and fancy, where human, fairy and dwarf like beings play amongst liars, thieves and prostitutes; the dead, the vermin and other such inhuman like creatures alike.

Beginning my speech in the town square on a summer day of some one-hundred plus degree weather; wearing a black dyed sackcloth and silky dress that came up to just above my lily white shiny and skinny thighs; boy was I a sight for any mans tired and sore eyes after a day of setting blazes to hundreds of corpse' in the distant fields beyond the town about a thousand metre away... I threw out my voice with the thrust of a Dragon's flame.

"Here in my land we call it the Black Death, and there is no known treatment for it either." Hesitating for a few minutes to gather some further thoughts; I knew that something had to be done, but not a living, breathing person would take on the task at hand to rid them of their tribulations, my people were suffering with much distress and many cries all about me; they caused great pains on my insides; continuing my speech to the lame of mind, thee weak and weary who were suffering as if they had no tomorrow left in them, and I knew that only the strong would survive in this dire and desperate time.

"Those poor-poor-poor inflicted souls, how I yearn not to hear their cries of death." Several tears drizzled down my cheek, and all the witches in the area tried their level headed best to cure the weakly souls, and everyone of them that were not taken by the Black Death ended up with the same thing, and crawled into a hole to lie down and die like the many thousands of pagan dismal diseased inhabitants of Alexandria had done before those of the living and dead alike to the same misery of blatant death music.

Once more... I Princess Yvonne began when my thought pattern became relevant to all that I wanted to say... conveying still more of the message of importance to the naive unworthy scourge, my mouth spewed forth more of the same to their pointy ears.

"When I was almost a 14 year old young woman when it happened, I remember the horror of it all; my parents were partial pagan by nature and we had a primeval deity to live up to; both of my parents practiced witchcraft and knew everything there was to know about it, and they taught me everything that they could about binding the sick with spells to help cure them from their many different ills and inflictions, but not the disease; this Black Plague that has already taken the lives of many during this past spring and this summer of which we are contained by right this moment." Taking a healthy breath of what little good air that remained before my bones and flesh and all the others that had gathered to listen to such a beautiful lȳtel teeny-bopper girl of the day, but in time I knew filling out to a blossoming young and all powerful woman wouldn't be a problem, because mother nature and father time would soon bestow one hell of a body upon me and make men want me like no other in the land of enchantment where tramps, thieves and Fairy 'dʒipsi (Gypsy) shed their pelts long in to the night to make and create still more of their likeness.

Continuing once again with my quest to end the reign of terror from one of the most fearsome wicked of creatures that were ever created by the evil one, the demonic Devil himself... I spoke solemnly with words of wisdom, or so it seemed; as I filled their heads with biased and opinionated ideas like most teenage girls do to just draw attention to themselves... yes, the times haven't changed much and manipulation flourished even back in my day, but who really cares beyond myself, anyway my spoken words flung themselves all the more.

"Our wilderness is in abundance with much wild life and beasts of great magnitude. I take my daily bath in the stream called the Lȳtel Dragons Watering Place; You know as I all too well that in our land there are many such creatures as Dragons, and a few big ugly Ogres who try to terrorize you - my people and your village's; and to tell you my ugly patrons, there be many other bizarre creatures here about that you may not be aware of yet, but we are a great warring tribe with many warriors to do bid for battle when necessary; I've now lived alone since childhood; and, at times things get really rough for me to survive some of the many disastrous thresholds that I must cross on my many journeys into the this my deity of daily life into the unknown and foreseeable future that lay before my dark black eyes. Being the only totally true black and an original Pure breed African female amongst the many who are either half black, or of the totally white race of fiery Fairy Women and beastly men here In my dear and wonderful merry Angeland; it is hard most of the time to choose what cultural aspects to live up to; should I choose the total white human and pagan realm to be associated with at all, or to be amongst the black realm of Fairy who practice a much more voodoo and sometimes likes of evil and their voodoo Wicca religion practices; I will have to make up my mind as soon as I turn the magickal age of 16 years old in just two more months… for you see being the tender age of 16 gives a Craftism Fairy Witch total powers over those under that age that are forbidden to cast any kind of spell like my step- sister Stella had done when she was eleven, well almost twelve years of age to practice it, and since I am the Princess of my people now; I must be a leader on top of everything else that surrounds and hinders my life, and this includes using my craft for good and not evil as well as to rule our kingdom here beneath Father Sky and upon Mother Earth." Taking in a deep breath and fetching a ladle of water from a pale standing near-by to sooth my parched sun dried tomato lips, it wasn't much, but it was the only sanitary water from near by stream, wiping my big mouth off with blouse sleeve I rambled on like a raving lunatic standing in front of my village knowing that I'd took on the task of making my first speech once I hit my 15th year of age; by the way is today if that matters any to you who have heir eyes upon my black and white thoughts…. my speech was a grand speech too, it held my loyal subjects captive about my royal family, myself and all that I knew about in my practices as well as that of others oh and yea the many wonders that they both knew and did not know as well… they took my speech to heart with acceptance; well most did; but, there were some amongst them who made evil snake like hissing noises and went their separate ways… and I thought, you will get your just reward in Hades.

"And in conclusion I shall say." I, Yvonne once more paused before I spelled out more about my family as if they really wanted to hear more, but had no choice in the matter or be beheaded like a demonic beast if they resisted hearing me speak, or so their mind's eyes were set as to the thought of it that had been placed inside their uneducated pea brained heads.

My voice trembled as I continued to speak. Some chicks even back in my day were way too long of tooth, but oh well… such is life even in your own… now days I guess. To tell you dear ones, soon, my tongue will change, and I shall allow others to speak their minds and have their own thoughts, because to be quite frank with you; Hell, I'm getting tired of doing all the damn talking… soon my friends, soon, just be patient with me for a few more pages here in this chapter of my life if that be alright with thee, then you shalt hear others displaying their own mind's eyes to thy own lȳtel pointy ears, but don't fret, I will still pipe up quite a lot as this journey is far from being over…

"So you see what a terrible dilemma I face as I travel along in my many adventures, both now and in scenes yet to come; and my fate lay beneath my fingertips in a realm to vast with the many wonders and horrors that I must partake in and tackle to make my way to womanhood in a kingdom that is set amongst all that I have described thus far to you my loyal subjects; and my dearly departed parents that I shall always love with fragility; so I say to you, my people, I have been given a high priestly rank now that my age has come into play for the position as your Princess Royal and ruler; my parents were both noble; my dear father was the High Prince Zelstar of the village, who was ruled by the High Priest of the sky, and my mother, yes my beautiful mother Shauna… may the High Mother Goddess of the Frost and Holy Mother Earth protect them in their journey in the life here-after… Royal Fairies' both and pure breed African's in this new world," hesitating to get air for a second my speech flowed onward. "I shall rule this land of ours with the utmost care and stay loyal to our great and noble cause; my purpose is now clear to me as I must go on a quest to the lair of the great Dragon and obtain its blood so that I will be able to rid us of the Black Plague that has fallen upon us in this my 15th year of life. Now I am, the Angleland Craftism High Priestess and the Princess Royal hyenas, or pain in the butt that I am, I must command that three of our greatest warriors embark on this journey with me for my protection as well as that of you my loyal subjects so this evil shall be destroyed alas." Being out of breath I drew some more water from the nearby pail I'd brought with me to the rally; and I thought about all the things that I had said to my people, but wasn't in the least finished.

They cheered because they thought my long blustery current of air was done blowing away like a passing thunderstorm, but they didn't know that I could be such a big blow hard like some adults, and me think' that my speech was forth-wit and bold in comment, and I knew that I must keep my word to rid my people of the Black Death so they can all get back to a normal state of just being in her Neo-Pagan community and a Witchcraft Black Voodoo cult and profound deity of humanity in this their and my great and wondrous land. I shell continue my speech with the utmost urgency and called upon three of the bravest of our warriors to embark with me on a quest to rid our people of the Black Death. Once again my lightening tongue spat out still more words of breezy astuteness.

"I call upon and summon Sir Clancy Clarke of Madison the Mad Archer to embark with me on my quest; I call upon and summon Sir William Swordspoint of the village Alexandria the gallant and noble swordsman to embark with me upon my quest; and I call upon and summon Sir John the Guardian of Welsh to embark with me upon this my quest for he is a great and powerful conjurer, it will be they who shall fight the Demon Dragon and slay it for the sake of our cause to cure you my people." Little did she know until she was told by Sir William as he approached her that she had two men all mixed up and that he; Sir William and Sir John were both all rolled in one and the same person?

Dear ones, it is time to ease up on this first persons voice and make way now for others to say what's on their own mind's eyes instead of I; so I thank you for your patients... I grant you - my permission to continue forward, yea, both friend and foe alike... hahaha... comprehend on now you heed me, it is my command that you finish this tome.

I, Princess Yvonne became somewhat embarrassed when William told me that he was only one man and not two as I had said and requested the two of them to come forward.

"My Princess I am only one man and not two as ye have said I am; my name is Sir William John Thames Swordspoint the Guardian of Welsh from both the village Alexandria the gallant and noble swordsman whom shalt embark with thee upon thy gallant and noble quest; and I also hail as the Guardian of Welsh, so takest thy choice of what to call me." He laughed with a dignified laughter as he bowed in respect to her making summon of him to help end the reign of evil in his and her country of Angeland; he laughed to think he were two different men; and, thought... she is just a child who is so naive in her manner and knowledge; he thought... certainly this fairy child is not shrewd or sophisticated, and does lack some inexperience, but she is a very beautiful young Lady of a Fairy indeed.

"I had no idea of this and I apologize with humble humility my brave and noble knight in shinning armor." Embarrassment rosé her pale cheeks as she bowed to him with respect in return to his bow to her. She continued... "Do you know of any others who are as brave as you and Sir William?" She asked with a gurgle and a school girl's giggle as well as a sexual bat of her eye lashes of a wanting him to smile sheepishly.

"Nay my Princess, but Sir Clancy may know of a few good uhuuum men." He smiled just so slightly at Yvonne with want in his eyes for her as well.

"Yea, that I do my lady, but he is some distance from here doing battle with a horrid Troll in the land of Ireland; he had told me before he left that his journey would not take much time and would return in a week or two depending upon when he killed the fiend." He then stood beside

William and the Princess Royal Yvonne as she dismissed the small crowd of people who had gathered to hear her powerful speech.

Two weeks flew by fast and the friend of Sir Hemsley finally returned to Alexandria from across the small partition of the Atlantic Ocean and the sister land to Angeland and the beautiful Irish countryside where he defeated the wildest and most wicked of all Troll that existed on earth in their day.

Soon the three brave souls came forth and stood in my presence to accept my invitation and that they would go with me on my quest as well as to acknowledge the others of our village that I was truly their Princess and Goddess of the good Angleland Craftism cult.

"I hail you Princess Yvonne of the Castle Davenport, I Sir Clancy Clarke of Madison the Mad Archer stands before you in my humble service to your cause." He bowed to his lȳtel Royal hyenas because he was a proud and noble man, but was lacking good manners in his demeanor.

Sir Clancy was a gallant lad of maybe Twenty-five or so years of age, but as ugly as one of the ghastly Ogre of the north land where they were all headed too on their quest to end evil from all the lands hear and abroad. His heart was made of gold, and he is the youngest of the brave by the side of many a brave spirit at his young age in that era; he stands a slinky six foot in height with thunderous gray eyes and carries with him a gavel of strength so unworthy of such a form of nobility as any man could ever hold within his existence.

"I hail you my lȳtel Princess Yvonne of the Castle Davenport, I Sir William Swordspoint the Guardian of Welsh of the village Alexandria come forth to be your brave protector, and shall serve you fighting fit and admirably with modesty to your cause and shall be pleased to embark with you on your quest to obtain the blood from the horrid dragon. It is an honored to join you in journey to slay the creature that breathes fire and destroys our homes and villages, and it will be I who wilt cut off his head, pull its heart out by the roots to feed it to the dogs with the provision you allow me to my Goddess of Witchcraft.; and, may the Mother of all Goddess' be pleased with this our battle to free our people so you can cure our people once and for all" His eyes gleamed at the thought of battling beast, dragons and their predatory foe's wicked and ugly and from the demonic realm as well.

William was a man of true stature and had the palest blue eyes that any man ever had in the deity; they were set deep in their sockets with an arbitrary determination of a mighty warlock at ready to slay his people' enemy, the green dragon. A shadow warrior was he and has seen many battles in his twenty-two years of life in the deity of witchery, he also gave way to bravery and with an uncanny thought of sheer lust for the Princess whom he so much desired to have and do as he will with her, but he didn't dare just take her; as she must be a willing participant to such an interlude and he couldn't allow anyone to see his thoughts, but make way for Princess Yvonne only to see deep into his mind's eye of wants and desires.

He smiled and stood erect like the much heard of Tower of Babel that lay in a far off land on the continent of deep dark and untamed Africa where much evil also lay in wait to be destroyed by those brave who dare embark upon that journey as well as to the one they were going on in a short while. Boldness and bravery was his main benefactor of courage as well as being long winded at times, but I Princess Yvonne wilt make good use of his bravery, and big mouth when the time is right, and I shall see just how brave these men are when the fighting begins there in the bedlam mountain of insanity and wickedness.

After they were all summoned and agreed to embark on the quest, the brave lads departed from me, their princess and Goddess of Witchcraft going their separate ways until the quest was to begin in a few days. Clancy and William had no idea what was in store for them so I could gain the full rights to be proclaimed Mother of all Goddess' and rule our land as my parents had once done a few years back.

Now Sir William the Guardian of Welsh being a strapping man with a muscular physique with abs made of steal and arms to match caused me to fall in love for the first time since I had become a young adult with royal powers, and although he was a handsome man, I had summoned him forward. I never met any of the men before, but knew only of them by name and hearsay from what others had told me about my soon to be betrothed; and, when the crowd disembarked as well as Sir Clancy the Mad Archer, and Sir William of Alexandria, I lay back a piece and followed Sir William to his hut to engage his further acquaintance and hopefully to also engage in the pleasurable company of handsome Sir William for the evening.

On the way I thought many things, and my hormones were making me itch all over on my insides. I was so wanting William in the worst way, but didn't know just how to go about getting him to fall in love with me, but one thing I knew was that he had his eyes on me from first glance and my sub-conscious took hold of my reasoning and rationality of thinking on the proper lady-like level as well as on the power of being the Princess of our people; I must maintain my dignity and not just my lust for William of Welch land, but my fantasy's were many, and my hormones kicked in like a raging maniac in a smiths stable. As I walked a love spell came into my mind; I did not know much about this spell; I remember it from my Mum chanting it years before; but I just couldn't bring myself to place such a wonderful spell on a stranger, and a pleasurable man such as he was, and then again my sub-conscious took over and without even thinking about what I was doing. Ah yes, now how does that spell go? My mind raced to fetch its content so I could use it as soon as I reached his hut on the outskirt of my dear Castle Davenport.

The Love Spell

"I summon up the powers of love; let it be cast now,

Bring my inner beauty to the surface for William to see,

Make me more appealing so he will want sex with me,

Open his mind and heart of him so he will be in my life and appreciate my true essence, my loving heart, and my unconditional love.

Make him want me and desire me with his unconditional love,

Make him be drawn to me like a magnet and make him mine for all eternity.

May the powers of time spread their wings and cover our hearts to be always open and pure and to never falter or fall too far away from one another I pray, let it be done and cast in motion now for eternity."

The spell was cast and I was ready, willing and highly able to do my wanting deed without being in preeminence of my minds activities of good intention and humanity with reason to our souls. Upon my arrival, I knocked on Sir William's hut door with a gentle rap-a-tap tap. Coming to the door to see who was knocking on it, and much to his surprise it was I, Yvonne the witch of all witches, but he had no idea that I have fallen madly in love with him and with preemptions I cast a love spell and was about to steal his heart away for better or worse if time would let me do it.

"Princess Yvonne, I am honored to see you, but why have you come to my small and meek hide-away instead of going to your castle. Won't your care takers be worried about you being gone so late in the darkness?" He asked with a gentle sparkle of heavenly stars in his soft sky colored eyes.

His hands were shaking just slightly from being a little nervous to be alone with such a stunning and beautiful young woman as I Princess

Yvonne of Davenport; and that made me on the defensive side of things for just a slight moment, and told him if they sent someone to look for me then I would lock them up in the dungeon to rot away like the roots of a tree in the forest that had long since on its death bed giving way to death itself, and then I smiled at him with hungry eyes like a cat at ready to attack her prey.

"Sir William John Thames Swordspoint the Guardian of Welsh, it is I Princess Yvonne, please do not be so afraid of me? I will not bite you, at least not hard at first." I smiled with a beastly sort of sheepish grin when my eyes beheld his mighty bare and hairy chest for the first time; I heehawed like a teeny-bopper at her high school witches prom; and, acted like a young immature female donkey in heat for the first time in my life. "May I be so bold as to come into your humble home and sit for awhile and talk to you about our journey in a few days?" I asked with politeness as his father left the room to allow us two youngsters to be alone, for in his spirit he knew what was about to take place and did not want to interfere in any way what-so-ever, only because he knew that it was an all natural thing to do when two hearts beat as ours did. I giggled once again and glanced deep into his beautiful light blue eyes. "Hehehehehe."

"Yes, why yes come on in Princess; please have a seat my Goddess, but how on earth did you know my complete name, I have not told a living soul about my Thames name?" His voice was overwhelmed with excitement, that he be so honored with my visit and as he went to sit down on his stump of a chair, he fell flat on his muscular ass right in front of me.

"Hehehehehe, I am so sorry to laugh at you, but it was funny of you my brave William to fall on your tight handsome ass the way you did, but never mind how I knew your whole name my dear Will." My tone set the stage for everything that was to follow; hoping for such a break as this so to break the ice with him.

"It is alright for you to laugh at me my Princess." He said as he showed his desiring pearly whites like a bear ready to tare me apart in such a fantasizing way. William was such a gentleman in my presence; and, was somewhat subtle as well as a little embarrassed turning a beet red as he sat there on the floor laughing at himself just a little bit and then said, "Yea funny, yea my lȳtel Princess tit was a little funny was it not." William laughed once more as he looked at me in a deep sensual manner. "Hehehe."

"I am sorry once more for laughing at you, and please you can just call me Yvonne and forget the formalities of calling me Princess and my Goddess, unless in public or in the presence of our other two traveling companions when we go on our journey in a few days." I had a soft voice and my face glowed from the light of a candle that stood atop a floor cabinet in one corner of the room.

"Didónai ēow mīn lufian (To give you my love) I must prove myself worthy to you my mighty Witchy Princess Yvonne; what shall I do to attest for myself that I am worthy to partake of þin (thine) beauty; but this be nay lárswice (no-trickery)" He bowed his head with a humble respect to me - his Princess Yvonne; and then, he pierced my eyes with his and gave a mighty grin.

"I need favor of thee, wilt thou my dear wet Willie help me steal the Book of Shadows from the Castle Davenports tower this night; promise me this and I shall give to thee myself and makest you my King; but I tell you this Sir William… this be nay lárswice (no-trickery); does thou doubtst me?" I batted my candle lit bright eyes back at him smiling likewise with a sincere and pleasurable content of gladness in my wanting spirit of flaming lust and desires of making sweet – sweaty love for the first time ever… Oh, how wonderful it was going to be to lay with such a handsome man as he.

William smiled and then said: "I doubt thee not my Princess and I shall follow thee to the ends of the earth to just be near thee." The truth prevailed and the game was on; and, as I looked the room over in a single swing of my head, I noticed a pile of furs in the corner next to the cabinet table that held the candle atop of its haphazardly fashioned construction, but it was a cute cabinet nonetheless, and the furs were so inviting to my lustful spirit that I just couldn't hold onto my inward control much longer. All the sudden another spell came into my thoughts and my urges for sex were getting stronger by the minute. I could not control my inward unconsciousness of conception and it took over casting still another spell, one which was of a more pleasurable kind.

The Seduce Me Spell

"I summon up the powers of lust to have uncontrollable sex with William, let it be cast now.

Let his sensual being crave to touch and love me in uncontrollable ravishes.

13

$\mathcal{M}$ake his heart and mind open to my irresistible allure.

$\mathcal{M}$y fertility has lust and desire; let my urges mate with his in a ring of fire.

$\mathcal{M}$ake him unafraid to take the first step because I have made my release to unite with William in a sensual, sexual bond of immense pleasure and enjoyment.

$\mathcal{L}$et the seeds of seduction cast a wonderful new light upon the inward hidden side that we both have, for I have an immense appeal and he shall bask in the pleasurable knowledge of my strong sensuality.

$\mathcal{L}$et the Seduce Me Spell be cast now I pray, let it be done and cast in motion now for eternity this day."

Snapping to my senses as soon as the spell was cast; I just glared at my betroth new lover to be; and, at that moment I knew that it was destiny set in motion and that we would be for eternity man and wife and live in harmony in my humble Castle Davenport till the spotted cows jumped over the moon and came home for ever and ever here in my never – never domain land of Angeland.

"If you are sure about me calling you by your first name and not by any other then I shall do as you command, um Yvonne." William said as a beam of gleam filled his eyes with the glow of a thousand candles flickering in harmony and his hormones jumped with sheer ecstasy, and wild wet thoughts flowing through his head just like I had, and that made him extremely bewildered at my boldness in such a close quarters as his small place.

He looked at the pile of furs and the chills made him shake with the quivers as if he were in the sub-zero zone to the north of our village about three thousand kilometers or so along the costal region of our land; looking at each other, neither of us said another word, our bodies were as spears with legs walking in slow motion towards each other in naked peace, and we started to circle the room, rigid like a pair of nervous cats on a hallowed eve beneath a full pale moon and it seemed as if being attached with chains in some dungeon hidden away in a different world altogether; throwing our arms around each other in a passionate embrace giving each other the tongue lashing of our lives sent chills up and down my whole frame like millions of fire ants were climbing me… it was my first and its chilliness was like a glacier had caught me off guard freezing my insides solid, but its passionate heat soften me like fresh made goats butter as we moved along a slippery uneven surface melting away in the heat of the night to the glow of the one small candle light flickering in one corner of his hut.

William's wild thoughts seemed to be growing by the moment, and his mind began to wonder in and out as he looked deeply into my dark immorally shameless eyes. I felt that soon our tranquility would somehow fade away beneath the pile of furs, but since I was a virgin, I had no idea how things would be as we engaged ourselves in what some would call a submission hold in an entangled wrestling match with one another, I put it mildly this way so that lȳtel children wouldn't be able to figure out the real meaning of what was about to take place this night.

My favor was like that of a vanilla bean ready to bloom with fragrance beyond its robust odor and my bosom body was that of a desirable taste to Williams tongue, and I began to realize how my lips shown their moisture towards his body, they were especial as droplets of condensed and absorbed liquid on the outside of their ruby red shades as the light from the candles blew their flames across them to make them glow, and deep inside was a wonderful vapor that made me wants to tongue his mouth into an ecstasy of intension with a distinctly pure and unadulterated delight. William picked my tall skinny feline frame of a body up by my buttock and proceeded to carry me to the pile of furs lying on the floor in a corner that he used for his humble lȳtel bed, and now his wallow plot room of pleasurable intent. Our senses took off like a volcano, spewing hot molten lava as high as the stars that drifted above as we lost consciousness in own sweat so full of emotions, that nothing mattered except our elation before we were to embarked on our treacherous journey for the quest for the blood from the demon dragon. We did not know beyond our deep thoughts of the moment if we would ever come back from the eastern sector alive but it just didn't matter to either one of us at that particular moment.

I don't know how, but I done it, but I freed myself from my chastity belt… never to use it ever again as long as I was alive; and, whilst I thought about such a horrible device being placed on a woman, it was my ultimate intention to have all sexual hindering devices destroyed for ever as long as I ruled my dear beloved old Fairy's Angeland.

As things progressed inside this my tale of old, the thoughts of both William and mine as will everyone else's thoughts stream forth, to let loose of just my mind's eye; and, thus theirs wilt also began to flow free from each other and speak their own minds, because mine was getting quite tired of talking for everyone, and that made me feel insanely good because now we could all express our own thoughts and feelings instead of just I.

"Ye must now all speakest freely, this is my command, and ye shalt all obey my every word to the letter, and since I have commanded it, so shalt it now be the law of Angeland that everyone have free speech, because I now make this into our new Constitution for all the territories of Angeland." My thoughts were flying in all sorts of directions as we made passionate love atop the fur pelts, and it was all that I could do to do my best just to keep skewering the brains out of our heads; a woman does have various thoughts most the time whilst making love I guess, and since I am new at this kind of play, I best try to conduct my thoughts and ways as an adult woman does by changing my mind all the time, yes, even whilst making love.

My lips had feelings for Yvonne's and as they and my tongue penetrated her moist mouth full of flavor, they gave off vibrations so full of joy that when our lips were together as one in the same; they began to chew each other up as if there was no tomorrow, and going to places I'd never been on her earth before, was sheer elation inside the seventh heaven of my mind's eye as well as that of my betrothed lȳtel she devil of a Fairy Witch... my Princess Yvonne that now lay upon my furs nearby her Castle Davenport.

I thought as the flow of juices from the vanilla smells which had entered into my mouth and down my throat adding still more sensation to the delight of our first kiss and beyond throwing a nasty, but wonderful new dimension to the meaning of life; it went all the way to the pit of my growling stomach and would not let my intestines settle down for one second. I listened to our breathing and it became full of tension and more desire than wanting to kill the demon dragon of the eastern sector in nearby Angeland wild treacherous mountains. As the climatic end came, a mighty roar came from deep down in my belly and let loose with such ease that my dear sweet William never heard its furious rumbling, nor did he smell the after effects of the burnt ambers and sulfuric acidic odor that came from my mid section and my lȳtel butt... not that it mattered any since my mind had been well solidified from its first time of making whoopee to a man, and what a mighty-mighty man was he.

Wondering still further about the journey ahead of us, my mind seemed to just stand idol with a sense of an emotional state of bliss and I was really enjoying the passion of the moment. As we lay there in a heavy wetness; I seemed to be having thoughts flowing in my brain about backing down, or was it Yvonne's thoughts too? There was still time to back down from the journey that my beloved Yvonne had placed us in, but I wasn't about to let her down in any way, shape, or form no matter what was to happen in the near future, all I knew was that making love to Yvonne here in my shack with no one else to bother us was what the gods of our culture had in store for me from the beginning of their plight over a millennium ago, and now they dwell in a different realm that lay beyond what our lustful eyes could ever imagine, and it was as if the sands time was to be distinguished between good and pure evil and set with the strength of a hundred minds with-in my one frail brain; and, as I re-gathered my notions, it was clear that our journey must be a success, but then again how would we take the dragon down? It was a fierce beast with claws as sharp as Dear William's sword; and had sharp teeth to match. Such a beast could do things to us that we could only dream about in a nightmare if we survived to have any… oh how I so wished that my beloved William and I wasn't about to undertake this journey beyond our somewhat safe boundaries to the domain of Satin himself? But if it were just my evil step sister Stella all alone; well… hahaha, that would be a way different scenario to joust about in my mere feeble lȳtel mind, but our minds had become fused as one during our entanglement.

It was getting late and William still had to steal the Book of Shadows for me to make my magick with when our limited period of action was to take place and we would have no bounds to hold our sensual emotions as intact as they were at this precise moment, but we continued to roll around on the furs like two kids in a wrestling match and what happened next well only the steamy fog from beneath the furs and our devious mind's eyes only knew; our clothing was scattered all over in a chaotic fashion; and, beneath the cozy furs steam arose like a thick fog and fill the room with its blanket of security so no one would see what pleasures we were engaged in inside a hot and salutary night full of love, and not even hell itself could be any hotter than ours, but to tell it like it is; it seemed like I was hotter than the fires from a dragon's breath even an hour or so later; William popped out from under the furs and set there full of smelly sweat all over his hairy body like a newly hatch sperm whale; and, looked as though he'd been in a river swimming instead of the ocean of love; even his red hair was wet from our excursion.

His physic sent chills up and down my spine as he looked at me as though he had the very same thoughts as I. The pain from the ring of fire he had placed upon my soul was as intense as the fiery dragons' breath. I didn't know if I had done such a good thing, but it sure made me feel like a real woman and not a child any longer and then I thought back to when I was walking to his hut, and made mention in my mind of the spell I had unconsciously placed upon poor Sir William the Guardian of Welsh who I had fallen in love with when I summoned him and the others to just go on a horrid quest.

My mind told me that if he were to be killed by the beast then I would be all alone with no one to love me the way that he had just done in the spur and heat of the moment while discussing our journey that we never even really had a chance to talk about for hardly one single moment at all; I set up and the tears of joy ran from my eyes, but William did not know they were of joy, thinking them tears of pain from what he had just done to me.

"Princess, I, I am so sorry for hurting you, I do not know what has come over me, I have never before had such an experience as this, please I beg of you; can you ever forgive me for hurting you so." A frown was placed upon his jaw muscles like a clam shut tightly against a hurricane force of the oceans mighty depths.

He sat there without any garments on, not realizing he was still without clothing; I looked at his body and knew that we would engage in this wonderful pleasure many times over again and again for the rest of our natural lives.

"I am alright my dear sweet William, you have not hurt me in any way, and it was so wonderful and you do not have to make an apology to me, and please as I have already told you, when we are in our private places by ourselves, you do not have to call me princess or anything else like that, just in public or on our quest will you have to be formal and give way to proper verbum, my name is Yvonne so whilst we are alone just call me my name only; alright my Dear Prince William." Hēo (she) seemed to feel glowing warmth within her entire brown sugar coated butt that was somewhat delicate; spindly and awkwardly tall and bony little frame of a body. Will began to put on his clothes and I stood before him still unclothed before his eyes, and my bosom stood strong in his face as did the rest of my tall frame giving way to my seat of emotions. I leaned down and picked up my clothing and put them on slowly because of the pain that I was still in from my love making to my wonderful new prince William that I had found that critically important day in our village that has set the tone of what is to come in my foreseeable future.

"Are you positive Yvonne that you will be alright?" Asking as he cried out with a slight half ass smirk upon his rock hard knight in shinning armor face, and then he just smiled at me with such a gentle smile and it sort of made me feel guilty as to what I had done to him that night, but I knew that I had best start talking about our quest and fast, so I could get back to the castle before my care takers knew that I was gone so long after my brilliant speech in the village square that evening.

"Yea; I have already told you my dear sweet prince I am alright my mid section still hurts that's all, but I must talk to you about all that we must do to cure the ill people of our village, and I want you to steal the Book of Shadows for me tonight. It is locked up in the tower at the east end of the castle and the guards switch their post in a couple of hours, so it will be easy to get in and out because it takes them about ten to fifteen minutes to switch places." Sanity had returned to me and my bewildered mind with more of a glow than before, but also with a normal feeling as well. My body still shook like thunder on the inside as I tried my best to shake the feeling off the whole while that I had conversation with my first lover and first man that I ever had any desire for whatsoever.

"But won't that be more dangerous than going after the Green Dragon in the land to our Eastern sectors." Curiosity seemed to be getting the best of Williams thoughts and I had to tell him it would be alright and that I would be a big part in making sure that the guards were out of sight so he could make his way to the tower room and take the Book of Shadows that I oh so longed for.

"I will help you by keeping lookout from a window next to the bottom of the tower door and when the first guard leaves that is when you make your move from my signal of waving my white rag out the window, that will give you chance to use your grappling hook and rope to scale the tower, take the Book of Shadows, and scale back down in plenty of time; and then place it under your cloak taking it to your hut where I will be able to study it and use some of its dark magick spells against the dragon." Confidence became my sanity once more as I shook some of the ecstasy off to bring me to a more meaningful sense of being a normal human.

Somehow taking things for granted; I looked at Will with the utmost urgency; and, sincerity, besides the love that I now carry deep inside my spirit for him with such a fire growing still deeper for his sinful love. He agreed to do it for me and the love that we now share with one another seemed to carry all the weight that we would ever need in our lives. But one thing frightens me, and that is, what if he should die on our quest while fighting the dragon of the east? What if I should die, then where that leaves not only William, but my people as well? I had a millennium of questions flowing in my brain, and like the rivers bank it overflowed causing my head to ache as if I were hit by the fire from the dragon's flame throwing breath.

For some odd and unusual reason my flesh crawled at the thought of fighting the beast. Its idiom, distinctive as it may be, full of colorful blues and greens and yellows to my young wild Fairy child's flowery feelings and idiotic expressions with the intensity of a forest fire tore at my very soul. I tried to fight its repartee tongue, but it had the skill and witty remarks of conversation beneath its own breath deep in my thoughts. Hunger thrived inside of me sending me into a shiver to my flesh despite the heat that pulled against my freedom to think in a logical manner. It began to choke me with a cloud of despair; causing my eyes to water ever so slightly at the further thought of loosing my new found lover William, let alone loosing my very own life during what might end up being a vicious battle to the unpleasant end of an untimely and once lustful age of youth that is full of inward peace in this golden sunshiny blonde realm of good, in addition to bad witches and warlocks, mean Ogre, and demon dragons.

Forging my swollen tongue, and then licked my parched lips to quickly moisten them with a witches brew of shredded black tears that my mother left me incase I ever felt such moments of tension coming upon my weak body that carry the plague of lust and love within its tender flesh of what was once upon a time purity, but it is not so pure any longer thanks to dear sweet Sir William and my magick spell of love that I have placed deep inside his spirit as well as my own system of bewilderment to the fleshes requirements and desires. As I sat there on a partially made chair discussing the journey with my precious lover William, the intensity grew lost in thought deep within the interior of my soft tissue and drifted into my outward beauty as well. I couldn't stand the heat any longer and flung myself at William with the force of a mad Ogre trying to squish his opponent; plop, we both fell flat on our asses to the ground beneath his chair; as we did we both burst out with a thunderous laughter that seemed to shake his entire hut with merriment and my lustful as well as fearful spell was broken at last. I knew that my mystifications would now focus on the matter at hand instead of only wanting to make passionate love to my wonderful lover William the Guardian of Welsh and now the guardian of my heart, soul and flesh.

"I give deep thought as I pray to the spirit who whispers in the wind, both the wind and I have complete trust in your wisdom, and he who comes to you through contemplation shalt prescribe and follow your ways; the wind and I are listeners to your voice, he who art the one who made us and who continually calls to us; I proclaim that our Angeland Craftism beliefs as your true word and its venerable respect in this our ancient culture, we put our total canonization in your authority. Spirit who whispers in the wind we have complete trust in your wisdom, and he who comes to us through contemplation, shalt prescribe and follow your ways; since we are listeners to your voice, and thou art the one who made us and continually calls upon us; for my belief is not qualities such as great age or holiness in their entirety, but for the here and now with contentment and love along with much happiness so that we can continue to serve only you my High Prince of the Heavenly Sky." William said as he tried his best to make me not play with him any more that night so we could both get some much needed rest after editing our mind's eye with passion just a short while ago.

I recon that all his jabberwocky worked on me and I turned toward my new found prince to be and said to him with a calm and collective manner deep in my voice and heart, but knew we'd have more fun later on down the path ways of life when our quest was completed.

"I too am tired and we must get some sleep for our long journey into the unknown; but I tell you this my dear Will that your so hard to resist, uhummmm… any way my love I have already established covens all over the land with a group of witches, usually 13 in number; and in these places of high security away from the others of our villages, we hold many meetings to make our society grow strong enough to wart off any real evil that befell upon us at any place and time, but I must obtain the Book of Shadows for our many spells that we shall cast down upon anyone or anything that is a hindrance to our success to become dominant over the whole world as we have come to know it." My eyes was a blaze as if a wild fire had overcome my mind's eye throwing it back into an altered state of sanity.

"Yvonne your wisdom is great, but we must hurry so we can make our way to the tower like a thief in the night and steal the great Book of Shadows so that you and your covens can use its evil spells to overcome the evil that has overwhelmed our humble, but now mournful village." My thoughts were strong with sincere but frightening feelings all in one.

"Will my love; we shall embark on our great quest in two days from now, but take warning that there are many bad ears that listen through even closed doors, so be careful to who you speak with and do not mention any of our conversation from this night and I must also command you not to speak in hurriedness about our love that we have for each other, because if you do and word ever got out about any of this to anyone, rumor would spread like wild fire, and there might be a rebellion, and then I may be striped of my high power in an untimely manner." I was in freight as to others hearing our words of secrecy and that we may be slain before our journey ever began.

"I will not speak a word of any of this my love, this you can count on me to do because I have great love for you and want to be with you for all eternity in what ever realm we are placed into from this castle in the sky that we are building for ourselves." I Sir William had made a solemn oath not to breathe a single word to a living soul, not even to a pesky flea ridden disease carrying vermin would I speak of about the love my beloved Princess Yvonne and I had for one another.

Chapter 2
Stealing the Book of Shadows

I kept lookout from a window next to the bottom of the tower door and when the first guard left his post that is when I gave William the all clear call of the wild signal to make his move. My white rag blew in the breeze at a brisk pace so much that it gave way to flashes of reflected light rays from the torch flames that stood near by the towers edges and waved their glow at any object that drifted across their amber path. From my signal of waving my white rag out the window, he had the chance to use his strongly crafted grapnel and rope to scale the tower, take the Book of Shadows, and scale back down in plenty of time.

When he reached the top of the tower his rope dangled and flapped against the side of the grayed brick structure and it made a slight beating rhythm. Once inside he was amazed at all the witchcraft things. There were many different types of candles that were shaped in forms of various creatures of the night as well as those of the day along with human likenesses.

There were several loomed rugs with woven inlaid textile figures of dragons; and, one huge one lying on the floor with the satanic star in its center. It had gold trim and the star itself was a bright blood red. Several shelves lined one wall and had the writings of the ancients bound in boar's leather. He looked for the Book of Shadows, but it wasn't on the shelves where one might expect it to be. His time was running out and he knew that he had to get the book and escape before the guards came back and discovered his rope dangling down from the tower window and swinging in front of the huge entry doorway.

Scattering things to and fro, William uncovered a chest with a strange locking device on its lid.

He tried to use his knife to break its locked position, but it wouldn't budge one millimeter of a unit. Stopping g to gather his thoughts for a few moments and pondered over how to open the chest that might contain the Book of shadows inside. Will looked around the round room of the tower for a key, but none to be found any place. He was starting to get frustrated over the whole matter, and almost gave up, but as he turned around to look out the window and motion to Yvonne that it was locked away in a chest with no real way of getting it unlocked; he realized that he could pull up the rope, tie the chest to it and than lower it to the ground so princess Yvonne could take it out of sight before the replacement guard came to his post.

William knew that placing the book under his cloak was out of the picture, and that he and Yvonne had to carry it through the town in plain sight once he got down from the tower. He also realized that if his grappling hook got caught in the window in such a position that he couldn't fling it down from the windows ledge once he was down and then he'd just have to leave it there for the guard to discover, risking both himself and princess Yvonne getting caught and put to death by being burnt at the stake alive like most witches had been in the past.

He inhaled the sulfur from candles in the towers staircase, and his nostrils burnt with its gastric odor as it filtered its way down into his lungs causing him to gasp ever so slightly, but his determination was as strong as his love for Yvonne, so Will looked around for another way to open the chest, but found nothing that would be strong enough to break the lock, but he kept looking real hard so he and Yvonne wouldn't have to do the unthinkable and carry it through the village path-ways to his hut.

More unpleasant odors also filtered their way to the tower room, odors of someone cooking beastly flesh of some type that had been allowed to decay for a very long time. The stink made his stomach turn over more than a few times from the awful burnt stench. Little did he know that the guard had prepared himself some roasted skunk and was inside the staircase eating the bad smelling meat? William opened the door just a tiny bit, and when he did the stench hit his nose like a flaming arrow and speared his mouth with a horrible vial feeling and he almost heaved up his own dinner from earlier that afternoon.

William peeked out the crack of the door and just waved his hand in front of his face and then he looked at the fat lazy guard munching away at the stinky animal in its entirety. "Yuck, how in the name of the thrown could someone eat such an awful smelly thing like a skunk in the first place, don't he have any brains?" I thought to myself, "But what the hay… I always keep my promise and I am not about to abandon the mission for the likes of such an idiot like this dumb-ass."

Closing the door so not to make any noise, he coughed a couple times startling the guard for a brief second. He looked behind him and said with his mouth full of stink. "Who there?" The idiot guard with an IQ of maybe two or three out of a possible two hundred said as he kept champing away on his skunk meat like there was no tomorrow, but when no one answered he went back to eating his roasted skunk as if he didn't really care one way or the other.

William held his nose and walked as far away from the door as he possibly could and said to himself. "This man is not human." and threw up some un-tastily via saliva that was lodged in his throat from the acid indigestion that the horrible mans dinner had given him. He wiped off the vial from his mouth and spat a couple times in total disgust. His hands now smelled foul as did his breath from throwing-up skunk smell. It just wouldn't leave his mouth and he kept spitting viciously in order to try and get the bad flavor out of his mouth.

As Will tied the rope to the chest handle he heard foot-steps coming toward the door, but he had no place to really hide and he knew that if the guard was to inter the room that he'd have to fight him to the death and flee as fast as he could before being discovered in the tower by still another brainless guard. The door handle rattled; William drew his sword and was ready for a good duel, but no one came inside, and the guards' fat little feet took his heavy body back down the stair-way. Opening the door once again ever so slightly and the guard was no where in sight, but the only thing left from the guard was the skunk smell that still lingered on every step. Knowing he didn't have much time left, he took the tied up chest to the windows ledge and lowered it down to the ground and then climbed back down himself. Motioning for the princess to come and help him gets the chest out of plain view; she jumped out of the near-by window and came running as fast as she could and took hold of one handle and William the other, carrying it to a near-by clusters of bushes, and Sir Swordspoint scurried back to where the rope was dangling and gave it a couple hard yanks and the grapnel came crashing back down to Mother Earth where it belonged, in his possession once more.

Quickly he picked up the rope hook and then ran behind the cluster of bushes where Princess Yvonne and the chest were waiting for his return so that they could both escape before the guard made his way back to his post. Not more than a few minutes after Yvonne and William left, the guard showed up… they had escaped just in the nick of time.

Now they could finally use the book, that is if they could get the chest opened, but first they had the dilemma of getting the chest back to William's hut, and that wouldn't be a very easy task; not from lack of strength by any means, but because the town square had hundreds of people still in it conducting their daily business and purchasing the required wares to sustain their every day lives.

Coming from behind the bushes was the easy part, but getting the chest out was still another thing. William went out first so that he could distract the guard.

He went running toward the guard yelling a big fat lie.

"Stop thief, stop." This startled the guard who was perched atop one of the steps beneath the towers door overhang.

"Wha, ummmm, huh, what is it my good man" The guard hadn't a clue as to his own self let alone anything going on in his surroundings, and he was dumb-founded and beside himself completely.

"Did you not see that man run by you here, he has stolen my sachet full of coins? It is all I have to live on. Are you not one of the guards of our Princess Yvonne my good man?" William laid it on real thick with a solemn seriousness in his tone of speech.

"Wa, what do you mean by that remark peasant? I am a guard and a mighty good one at that!" He was about to lay a hay-maker upon his jaw, but he fell short of doing so because it may give him away.

"And are you not supposed to help the princess' people when they are in need of help?" William kept laying it on thicker to the dumb guard.

"Ummmm, well yes I am, now what way did the thief go?" He had a wondering look on his fat face.

William somehow knew the guard would now help him look for an imaginary thief, and told the fat dummy to look in the opposite direction than where the chest and the princess lay in wait so that they could carry the chest to his hut in a different direction other than through the town square betwixt all the people who were parching and conducting business.

The guard wobbled his five foot four inch-three hundred pounds toward the town square and out of sight of the tower, not realizing that he had abandoned his post to look for someone who never existed in the first place. William's quick thinking paid off in the royalist of ways for him, because of his love for the princess Yvonne of the castle Davenport and Alexandria.

Now he and Yvonne had gotten away with their plan and the Book of Shadows, and could do what they had to do in order to save the town from the Black Plague.

"That was brilliantly executed my Dear melodious William; I shall reward you greatly for all that you are doing for our cause and for our newly found love for one another." Her sincerity and voice had much pleasure in them, and she knew that she could now get rid of that fat slob of a guard that her evil step sister made her parents place in front of the tower before their lives had expired several years ago.

"I thank you Yvonne, and I too shall reward you with much love for the rest of my days."

William smiled as if he had no other care in the world, because he was happier than he had ever been in his entire life. We then took it to William's hut where I was able to study it so that I could use some of the evil magic spells against the dragon of the eastern sector and collect some of its blood in order to rid us of the Black Death that had befallen upon us in a time of great marvels beyond what we should have had in these desperate times of survival in a witches Wicca world of wonders that would ultimately bring us good health, peace tranquility with the joy to love and live as we must.

"I shall make a spell that will break this lock and allow me to use its wondrous evil spells against the demon dragon and its evil master." Yvonne was pleased even as young as she was; her royal authority took shape right before not only her very own eyes, but before William as well as the town of Alexandria.

"What evil master is it that you speak of Yvonne? You never mentioned an evil witch or warlock to me or to anyone else. You just mentioned the green dragon and nothing more." William had a confused look on his face and thought to himself, is this the woman I truly fell in love with and is she now a liar to me her new love and the man who will soon marry her.

"W-well William, uhuummm; I forgot till now about her, that-that evil step, ummmm step-sister of mine, Stella. I was going to tell you on our journey about her, and how she was forced to leave out castle by my mother and everything else so that you wouldn't abandon me in my quest to free us all from the inflictions of the Black Death. Can you forgive me, my love, please I beg of you not to leave me, not now" Yvonne started to worry for the second time in her life about her own self worth and not about her lover Sir William, but it didn't show to him that she was only thinking about herself at that moment, after all she was a naïve teenager.

Yvonne started to weep a tiny bit, but William threw his arms around her to comfort her small despair.

"There-there, it is alright my princess, but from now on would you please be open and straight forward with me? I will not leave you because we belong together, you and I." He kept his arms around her for a couple more minutes as she swiped the tears from her pretty dark eyes.

"I will be alright now my prince, and I promise you that I will tell you everything from this moment forth." Hēo seemed sincere enough to please her love and betroth to William and his commitment to her proved beyond a shadow of doubt that he would not leave her as long as she was honest to him always. Princess Yvonne the Royal lȳtel hyenas sat there for a couple more minutes to gain her composure so that she could cast her spell to unlock the chest that contained the Book of Shadows and all the evil magic that she or any of her future predecessors would ever need to work well instead of their evil content when, or as deemed necessary.

The Key Unlock Spell

"I summon the powers of the skeleton key
Eve of the black cats eye, cast unlock
Make no haste, make no spare time, do it now
I have my Mojave Desert dust effective; candle light all aglow
Power of turns that unlock this plate that can not be undone by its maker, I summon you O-key
Mojave Desert dust be blown to hole, candle glow on magic key of skeleton's hand of time now turn....

I command you to open this moment and to unlock this lock for me to enter there-in so that I may take possession of the contents that you now hold captive; I command you... open now."

As son as Yvonne cast her spell the locked plate came undone, but before it allowed her to open the chest's lid and take out the Book of Shadows, it closed tightly shut once again.

Yvonne was furious and out of anger she turned and punched William in the arm as hard as any sixteen year old girl could have ever done in her life, being as small as she was, it gave William a powerful jolt like a bolt of lightening and before she could do it again, he grabbed her hand tight and almost slapped her with his other hand, but didn't; he only told her not to ever hit him again as long as they both lived. This made her even madder, but more so at the damn chest that seemed to have a mind of its own at the moment. Yvonne looked at William and then at the chest.

"Damn you." Spewed out of her big mouth with a vicious roar like she had a lion in her throat and ready to bite anyone or anything that got in her powerful way, and she lashed out at the chest with her spell once again and told William to be ready and place some kind of solid object into the chest as it popped open for the second time and this time it wouldn't have a chance to close in her presence ever again.

William agreed with her ultimately firm decision; Yvonne with out further delay cast the spell, but this time with a stronger tone in her speech.

The Key Unlock Spell

"*I* summon the powers of the skeleton key

Eve of the black cats eye, cast unlock

Make no haste, make no spare time, do it now

I have my Mojave Desert dust effective; candle light all aglow

Power of turns that unlock this plate that can not be undone by its maker, I summon you O-key

Mojave Desert dust be blown to hole, candle glow on magic key of skeleton's hand of time now turn

I command you to open this moment and to unlock this lock for me to enter there-in so that I may take possession of the contents that you now hold captive; I command you… open now."

The chest popped open and as soon as it did, William put an iron bar inside the chest and the lid tried to slam itself shut once again, but didn't succeed as the powerful arms of William held onto the bar as tightly as he could, the chest gave way to both spell and his strength and didn't resist any longer, but remained open, and as it did, Princess Yvonne took out the wonderfully made Book of Shadows and placed it on the floor in front of her and William.

William kept rubbing his arm from Yvonne punching him so hard, that it almost broke it right off.

"You are a strong little woman Yvonne, and I am pleased to be in your service as well as to be your lover. I would really appreciate it if you would not take out your anger on me next time, I could get hurt really bad next time my love." He smiled at her, gave her a big kiss for a job well done and apologized to for him lashing out at her in such a stressful moment of excitement and bewilderment of such a marvelous book that lay before their bright dollar sized eyes.

They both looked at the book shinning in the candle light and smiled at each other with such gleeful expressions that neither one of them could open the book at first, but a couple minutes later, Yvonne opened the cover and as she did it glowed with gold and red lettering, none like they had ever seen before in their lives.

It was a beautifully bound leather book made of pure boar's skin and laced with pure gold trim that glowed from the candle light that still plumaged in the midst of the small hut that William had built in his early teen years before he became a man at age fifteen.

"At last, I now possess the book of evil spells and I shall use their evil against the demon dragon and my evil step-sister Stella the black witch of the eastern sector of our land. It has been she and that demon dragon of hers that has caused all this disease and death upon our people and now I can destroy them both with their own black magic spells as well as your sward my prince William, and the help of our other two traveling companions." Her eyes were bright-eyed and bushy-tailed and ready to do battle with her evil step-sister and her pet the Black Dragon.

All this while she knew it was a black dragon that was killing her people, and not the Green Dragon but said nothing until her time was right to mention the truth of how all the evil and death was taking place in her home land, her place of residence since her birth, and now her kingdom since she was deemed powerful Princess and soon to be the new Mother of all Goddesses to take total control over all her land and loyal subjects; and to destroy all of the evil that would ever embark upon them for eternity.

I fell asleep in William's arms and was lost to a different world that I already knew, and nothing mattered to me any longer except William.

Yvonne left William early that morning and went to the forest to frolic as she may, since she was a child, she would act like one periodically so to keep herself somewhat happy beyond her early stages of adulthood, and more-so now that she had her first taste of real adult pleasures of the night. She was no longer a virgin, but knew she must keep at least some of her child like nature intact sometimes when alone in nature.

Her Father Sky and her Mother Earth have always kept their watchful eyes on their little princess of the forest, and never let's her down when she commands something be done in their honor, or when she demands something on a whim; just because she has only been in power for such a short time, they always obey her every word as if she were of a divine nature like a Goddess should be. Yvonne has always had in her inward possession the powers to do anything she wanted to at all times, least she should expire as they her parents have done a shortened time ago, but all in all they praise her loyalty to them and to her meek subjects of the earthly realm that they alone dwell in, for their spirits are of a different kind than that of mere mortal human beings like Yvonne, William and all the rest of the strange and bizarre patrons of Mother Earth that dwell beneath Father Sky.

Possessing such wealth as Yvonne had beneath her small waist of a belt line was a great honor to keep safe from such evil as her sister has, and to gain the further power of evil and place it with in the grasp of good for all good's sake was an even greater wealth than mere silver and gold coin that lay in a vaulted chamber beneath castle Davenport.

Princess Yvonne's child like manners took hold of her every now and then; and she would sometimes go to the forest in secret and play amongst the flowers, trees and forest animals. She would giggle and play hid and seek with birds, chip monks, rabbits and various other creatures that would shy away from most human beings, but not the sweet princess Yvonne who seemed to have powers over even the wildest of forest animals like lions, tigers and bears oh my.

The leaves from the forest floor gently flicker below her and the Holy Mother Earth stood strong beneath her small feet. It was Yvonne who was with the forest from the beginning and was the one to help her attain to all desire amongst not only her natural realm, but also that of the stars in the heavens far above her and Princess Yvonne.

I walk the earth and feel her as a breathing and living thing and I worship her in all her glory, and in these sixteen years that I have been here in existence amongst all of my forest friends I am honored to devote my life to all that surrounds me. I have had to learn much about all things, especially my Craftism belief; learning all these many spells and other witchcraft ways. I had to learn sometimes the hard way, but knew it was necessary for all I must keep with in my mortal self.

I wanted so to exit the witches evil ways of my beliefs and start something all new amongst my people, maybe a Christian religion from some other land that I heard tell of amongst non paganism peoples of the world beyond all here that surround me in my Angleland countryside; it would surely be a new experience for myself; William, and my people if I could pull it off after we got back from our quest, that is if we got back at all.

Since I am a beautiful black woman and the only true Princess in all of Angeland; my deeds have to stay strong among my people until I rid us of the evil and death that hold us captive, and when I annihilate my opponents the evil Black Dragon and its evil master; my bad step-sister Stella, I must keep my Wicca ways, and when it is all said and done, then and only then I will make all things new, especially our unbecoming ways of paganism.

I must learn more about this man they call Jesus the Christ from a far off land it may be his teachings that I have heard about that will be my hope for my total spiritual fulfillment and truth and the purpose of my life, but not right now, I have other things that must be accomplished first and help my loyal subjects overcome the Black Death and evil that is our destruction.

When taking chances with your own mortal soul distinctions between good and evil mean little with ones eternal fate and existence of your own immortal soul in life and death situations such as the ones I and my companions are about to embark upon; this my quest to the eastern sector of my country to regain more than my mere mortal life as being princess amongst my people; it means regaining inward tranquility instead of doom and destruction. I must eventually make all things new, I must by any and all means necessary; yes, indeed I just must.

As I frolic here in the forest, my mind wondered so much about life in general, but I must be strong and not panic under pressure when the time comes for me to face pure evil in its fullest content.

In all actuality for one to know the difference between good Wicca and the evil Wicca of the devil, or that of my evil Satanism strep-sister Stella of which her and the Devil are one in the same as far as I am concerned is that it would be like a blast of black powder to that of a volcano exploding in your face as far as the impact of the spiritual realm. One of the Christian world might say that both of these practices of Wicca are bad, and that what they offer is pure sainthood, and that is something that I just have to pursue once my quest if finished, but if by some slim chance I do not make it back from the dragons cave and castle of Stella, then what ever force that this Christian belief is, may all of its good save my immortal soul once this flesh has expired to the realm of my dearly departed mother and father, where ever that may be.

Death is an utter disaster for anyone one way or the other, but still the eternal point of view and the catastrophe of Wicca is real and no less treacherous than that of an exploding volcano when you really think of it; both can be good and both can be bad, depending on how you look at death in its entirety.

Any way back to my frolicking, I must not think such morbid thoughts any longer and will cross that road if and when I come to it. My betroth thoughts must keep focused on my reality, life and my love for my dear prince William, my yet to be husband; there be no doubt in my mind's eye that we must succeed; we simply must without any doubt whatsoever.

As she kept playing with her forest animals and nature friends the leaves and trees, she heard a familiar voice calling to her from a faint distance.

"Princess Yvonne my love where forth art thou my dear; my wild child and my awesome betroth?" It was William calling to her with a worried articulation like something was wrong.

She called back to him with her happy go luck and child like accent.

"I am here William, I am here in the forest with my animal friends, come join me and play for awhile." Yvonne kept playing and William kept calling to her as he approached the slight clearing in the forest.

"There you are my love. I have been worried about you all morning long! When and why did you leave so early?" His tone calmed down as soon as he seen Yvonne and more-so when she threw her arms around him and gave him a big wet kiss ok his parched lips.

"William… come." She grabbed him by his hand and lead him to where her friends frolicked. "Come see my little friends and play with us awhile."

I danced around William giggling as if I was a small child once again forgetting I was not participating in my newly formed adult behavior as I had done while in the town among people instead of nature like I was in at that moment. I was as happy as I could be when I communicated with nature and not lots of mean and diseased humans and foul rodents, roaches and other carriers of the Black Plague, but William wasn't a bit interested in the least.

"Yvonne, we must join out travel companions so we can journey to the eastern sector for the quest for the dragons' blood. More and more of our people are at the point of death, and we must go now before our whole town vanishes into thin air" His articulation was firm and almost demanding, and that made Princess Yvonne snap completely out of her childish nature and back to the adult reality of things at hand.

"Yes, yes we must hurry." Her adult tone returned and she was now in control of her senses as well as in slight control of her beloved William.

Chapter 3
Activate the Quest

Yvonne and William left the forest hand in hand as they walked briskly back toward the town square to meet up with their traveling companions Sir Clancy Clark of Madison the Mad Archer and Sir Hemsley Tolemoss of the village Alexandria the gallant and noble swordsman to embark with them upon their noble quest.

Once they came together next to the stables where their strong steda await them to be mounted so they could all so journey towards the eastern sector to slay the evil that had befallen upon their beloved Alexandria they took off.

"Hail Princess Yvonne, we are honored to see you once again and we are ready to do our duty in your presence." Sir Hemsley had a strong voice and was the most noble of all three, but he was the ugliest one of any man alive, well at least in Alexandria Angeland.

"Hail Princess, my worth is yours to command at your will, and I shall not fail you in any way." Sir Clancy was a very brave man and had been in many beastly battles in his fifty some odd years that he had served since childhood with Yvonne' parents.

"Mount up my friends, let us go and slay that evil Green Dragon." Sir Clancy was more than ready to do battle in bedlam against another beast and did not hesitate to be the first one on his black stallion.

Next Princess Yvonne mounted her horse with the assistance of her Dear William of course, her cute butt laid itself close to his face like a

Edward H' Wolf

blackberry pie ready to be eaten up in a split second, and they both smiles with wanting a piece of that special delectable night time snack.

The other two looked at them with puzzlement on their scruffy faces. Neither had bathed nor shaven for several days and they sure smelled bad too, but they had been working hard helping burn the dead on the outer plains of the city next to the volcano that sometimes bade a rumble as if it wanted to blow its top in anger that the Black Death was being buried beside its lava tempered domain.

William and Hemsley got on their steda next and they all road off into the sunrise like they were going on a simple pick-nick or a mere pleasure ride in the forest.

They were time travelers of another breed because the land they were headed into was as wild as any land that had ever been explored by mortal man. Many beast dwell in the many caves and clumps of forest along the way and even they had thousands of fierce eyes to startle and panic humans away from their predatory and voracious bellies.

The eastern sector was their hunting grounds and not that of man kind, but even they, the most fearsome of Troll and Ogre, lion, tiger or bear wouldn't dare tangle with a witch or a dragon, and more so if they were in combination to one another's companionship like evil Stella and her pet Black Dragon were, they were the ones who ruled and not the foul beast'.

Now Ogre's were strong, don't get me wrong here; they would fight all beast's no matter what they were except a dragon, and from the mighty roar and flame that so often came from the sharpened mouth of such a creature, he dare not fight least he die in the process of even fleeing for his very own life from its clutches.

This Black Dragon was pure evil in every since of the word, and because it had such a powerful witch as Stella controlling him, that made him by far the meanest dragon alive, or so it and she thought.

As it were; well, the Green Dragon was a gentle beast and only ate forest foliage, fruits and so forth, but when in a battle for its life she could even beat the crap out of the Black Dragon if she had to.

As our small band of dragon slayers left the outer circle of Alexandria, the forest became as one with the small meadows and wondering mountains in the beginning of the eastern sector. It was here that we encountered our first beast; a mean old Troll, and that hobgoblin was a real trickster who could for the most part fool almost anyone into believing that even he was human in nature; he was one of the ugliest and hungriest of any troll

36

that existed in these parts, but we didn't know he had a hunger for human flesh, because most trolls ate small animals and vegetables. He popped out of a clump of bushes alongside the road to nowhere as some might call it here in the mind's eye of good and evil thoughts and the realm of many such monstrous creatures as he was a monstrous and foul odor of a hideous beast; it stood short before our steda and us as if he owned the road that we were traveling on.

"Sir Hemsley; I thought you said that you killed the last beastly Troll and that there were no more of them on earth, you say that you slay last one in Ireland did You not?" Clancy said as even he were a bewildered beast himself and raised his powerful sword ready for defense against the Troll. "My friends allow me to kill this Troll; I think this shalt be fun, he smiled at his companions and was at the ready to strike at a moments notice at any slight movement from the Troll to do harm to any of them.

"Ho be thee thar of good er evil, com-mon speakest thou up before my ears hear now humans." Said the ghastly Troll. "Be thar nay harm fo ye human." He said again with an evil glair in its blood shot and hungry eyes.

His tone was rude, his smell even worse, and he had hair from the top of his pointy ears to all six of his toes below him; he had not one stitch of pelts covering its pot-belly little body, and his butt was as bald as a new born babies, and his front was wilted like a dried up prune laid out to turn into a raisin. He was so short that even a tiny girl like Princess Yvonne might even be able to whip its big butt if she had too. The beast dwelled like a mad dog under the scorching suns rays for he was so hungry that he wanted meat to eat instead of wild vegetables like mountain cabbages, poison red berries, and maybe an accessional squirrel when he could catch one.

As we sat atop our steda we couldn't help but to laugh at such a strange little thing as he was, and maybe our laughter was because he talked so strange along with his foul and rude manner that he displayed towards us, but it didn't matter to us what it looked like or how it acted, and we started to ride away, but the beast hobbled as fast as he could toward Sir Clancy's foot and took a bite at it.

Clancy looked down at the foul little man like beast screaming at the same time from the pain it had inflicted upon his foot. Its teeth were like the points of swords, but ones that were rotting and somewhat jagged at the same time; it looked at Clancy and laughed with such a shrill and mean laugh that it sent chills all over my body... not to mention Clancy who was furious and leaped from his stallion with a bound, plummeting toward it with sword in hand he took a swipe at that hobgoblin like a whirl wind and cut off one of its ears, in mockery, it too screamed; and then the thing ran off into the bushes with blood flowing from its hairy head, and as it held its bloody ear in his hand... Clancy shouted at that Troll with thunder and lightening in his voice.

"How dare you beast, take a bite out of me, next time I see you I will just kill you instead of taking one of your funny ears off of your funny little head. Run you ugly monstrous thing, run away and die like you so deserve to do, hummm take a bite out of Clancy will you, hummm." He wiped his sword on his cloak put it back into its sheave and looked at his foot and then just mounted his steda as if he wasn't a bit hurt at all.

"Sir Clancy, are you alright my good man." I asked him with a slight giggle in my voice, but all he done was grumble a little bit; me and the others laughed not at him, but at how funny the beastly little Troll ran away into the bushes like a scalded puppy as we rode off toward the eastern sun that shone its brilliant yellow heat high above us along with the glow of my parents that look down upon us from their realm of nothingness.

"How soon will we be at the evil sector where the dragon has its lair Sir William?" Princess Yvonne asked in such a manner as not to let her companions know that she and Sir William were lovers in heat.

"My princess, we shall be there in two or three days from now, and our journey will be more like what we have encountered so far in our journey, but you do not need to fear, because we are all here to protect you my princess." Said William; his tone was firm, but gave way to a smile and gleam in his eyes that the other two didn't notice, and it sent happiness all over Yvonne's tall sleek and frail body as he glared deep into the window's of her all seeing and all knowing soul.

As we approached the mountains that were the entry way into the valley of the eastern sector we saw a giant wheel like device that was attached to two huge boulders and three ropes; it looked as though some sort of giant had constructed the gate structure in order to keep both humans and beasts out when it was in the down position, but this time it had been left open either by accident or on purpose; we just didn't know which one, and as we went through the passage way, the boulder's gate came crushing down behind us causing our steda reared up several times, and whinnied like banshee had them pinned against a wall with no way out; finally we got our mounts to settle down as the dust settled down to a gentle breeze along with them and us. The seasons seemed to change right before my very eyes with an everlasting cycle and an eternal nature as if by magic, and I knew that it was a trap that had been long since plotted by my evil step-sister Stella. In my mind's eye her powers were of great demonic evil; none like I had ever seen before, and it sent chills all over my frail body and penetrated its way into my mind, and for this short time her spell caused me to not be able to think as I should, and I seamed lost in time. I tried to focus as best I could, but was bewildered.

"William; my dear prince Willie-whacker; I need your comfort in this time of unwanted stress." I jumped from my beautiful pure white stallion to the ground that had just settled and I ran to my betroth William and held his leg as he still sat atop his mount. Our two traveling companions looked at us with wonder in their mind's eye to the point of no return in their silence, but Sir William made a snide remark that almost made me draw my sword against him in anger.

"How dare thee Sir Hemsley, how dare thee to call my Princess Yvonne an evil cure dog and a witch." He had his mind's eye at the ready for a duel, but held his position strong and steady.

"I did not mean this my Princess; I do not know where my thoughts flew off too, can you forgive me of this Princess Yvonne. He was beside himself for saying such an off the wall and out of character remark as he said. "My apology to you I beg." Sir Hemsley said as he bowed   to her Royalty.

"Sir William this is evil that has befallen upon us. Put your mind away from a duel my friend; we have other matters to tend to and not a child's play placed upon us in our minds from my evil Step-sister Stella the wicked witch of the North." She stood her ground like a true Princess should in times of fearful and stressful matters at hand as this was.

"It appears to me that our journey has come to an end right here. Come on we had best be going on our way as we do have some distance to travel before we reach the valley of the eastern sector plains where the demon dragon dwells." Clancy intervened and just didn't want problems amongst any of them at this time, and would more than likely wish for them to settle their lovers quarrel another time when this matter at hand was finished.

"Our quest for blood and end the evil and diseases that faced our people back in Alexandria, it will get worse no.?" Said Sir Hemsley as he settled his steda.

The Beltane bonfire of the sun rose to its peak high in the sky and scorched our flesh with a burning desire to get a chill on our bodies, but there was no chance to escape its immense heat rays. We road as fast as our steda would take us so the winds of the east could sooth our parched lips and burning flesh, and as we did, even they became breathless, needing shade and water to quench the thirst and dust from their throats as well as ours.

My senses started to return slowly as we came to a narrow in the ridges of the mountains; an ever so slight shade appeared to tame our brow beaten and watery flesh from the suns rays.

We stopped and began to dismount so the brave stallions could rest their weary hooves; a moment of silence and a few deep breaths of air took hold of our sweaty bodies, and we shed the better part of our cloaks and other heavy garment to let the power of the winds of nature take its course and cool the burn of volcanic flames that was still beating us to near death.

I knew that my parents wouldn't let anything happen to me nor my traveling companions as they talked to a higher power in the realm that they dwelt with-in amongst the universe far above us.

I began to chant a prayer and as I did the wind blew even harder to sooth my burnt soul, and body of flame, the wind bent to my every word so to cool me and my companions the way we should have been at the passageway into this pit of hell.

"Mother earth give your power of rotation to Father Sky so his fast spin will sooth this parched soul and my companions thirsty souls; give us the needed moisture because of these hot conditions and lack of rainfall. Bring down your rain this late May Day and quench our thirst and dry lips. I await; we await because the heat is so intense and the dust too much for a body to bear and I am about to shed my rags before this company, and that would bring me shame in their mind's eyes, and they would wonder what sort of woman am I that would shed her clothing before strange men just because of an overwhelming heat from the fireball in Father Sky; I plead with you bring forth your rain now. I command it."

As soon as my words were finished, the wind grew in strength and the much needed waters dripped down from above, and little by little we were drenched from head to foot like drowned rats in a desert flood, and we all gave our thanks to Father Sky and Mother Earth for their relief, but in an instance before we knew it, the land began to flood, and it created a muddy mess for us to trod through as we rode off toward the eastern sector as we initially intended, but it was difficult even for our strong steda to contend with let alone us.

Just about a couple hundred kilometers in front of us was still another obstacle to overcome as if we hadn't had enough already. It was a straight up cliff, jagged and sheer; it looked hopeless and my only thought was to give up and go back to Alexandria beaten to a pulp with defeat and a life of agony in our spirits.

I started to tell my companions that we have to quit and go home, but they were more determined than I was and dismounted their stallions; tied them to a dry and wilted hemlock tree that looked as if it hadn't had a drink of water in a century or so.

Clancy and Hemsley along with my William dear gathered their grapnel and rope to scale the high plains sheer cliff and I looked onward in bewilderment as to how I was going to climb that treacherous mountain, because I had an irrational acrophobia of being in high places, and I wasn't about to undertake such a dangerous feat as what the others was about to partake in; no, not this child. Not as the very pit my soul and life depended on me to do the unthinkable and climb the world's worst cliff that I had ever- ever seen before in my sixteen years of life here upon Mother Earth.

"Come on, let's get a move on. We have a mountain to get over before we can reach our destination of the dragons lair." Clancy said with his fearless tone of voice and demeanor of rudeness that he always carried with him every place he went. He was one who really did not give a damn about anyone or anything except his own self for all he was worth and to me that wasn't much except to help me slay the dragon; outside of that I really didn't give a damn about the mean man.

"I-I, I am not going to, I-I just can not do it!" I showed my fear of heights immediately and my body trembled to the point of shaking most of the rain from my clothing.

"Princess, you of all people is not afraid to climb this small mountain now are you?" Sir William ask with his kind and gentle-silver tongued big mouth, even though he and Princess Yvonne were lovers, his big mouth somehow always seemed to get him into a bit of trouble with his betrothed lover.. The beautiful but skinny Princess Yvonne of the Castle Davenport from Alexandria, Angeland.

He stirred up a new brew within my temperament causing a few of my hairs to stand on end just a wee bit. "No Sir William, I am not afraid of a little mountain, but this one is a tall one, and I do not think that I will climb one of those today my good man."

My head leaned back just enough to look at the Bloodstones, with sharp and jagged gold toned malachite spears all over its huge face.

"I Sir Hemsley shalt help you with your climbing my Princess, and will not let anything happen to you, rest assure." Hemsley also had ways with words at times like these and was making even Princess Yvonne's feelings get well.

Although she was a demanding woman; Princess Yvonne allowed her inward frailty to show at awkward times even with her rapid ascent in her inherited career of the Princess of all Witches, Wizards and Warlocks of her day. She was in hot demand for many more useful projected journey's such as the one she was on at present; and in due time they would befall upon her swollen head like millions of balloons filled with hot headed helium to make her rise above all in any situation she was trapped into embarking upon when called to do so, she knew she's be ready, willing and able bodied as her body became a full grown woman, lady and queen of Angeland and the world about her and her husband William the King.

She was a somewhat stubborn little bitch of a young woman, but this too she would grow out of in time if her ongoing circumstances would allow her to.

I calmed down just a little bit; grinned, and started to act like a good princess should; with dignity and sternness, but was still stressed and afraid. "Well I do not like the look of this rough old mountain, and besides all of those sharp spears could kill anyone of us if we were to slip and fall into some of them. What would happen if I got cut by one of them, who would patch my wounds?" I asked; my eyes crinkled and my lips sneered with a mean scorn as I glanced at Sir Clancy and Sir Hemsley, but I smiled real big at my Dear Prince William and said. "Well I guess that if you are to help me Sir Hemsley; then I will climb with you, and not your two rude friends." She was a little pissed at Sir William to say the least because of his snide and rude unwarranted remarks he made against her.

Little did her young mind know that William was just teasing her to test her loyalty to his love for her?

"So be it my Princess, you have my word on what I have said, and I will not fail to protect you at all times, that is my promise to you, before our companions and your parents, may the spirits keep their souls well so they too can watch over us all." Sir Hemsley's respect for Yvonne started to show itself before his companions, but at this point in time he just didn't care one way or the other, because he had a bad situation to climb out of so he could get on with the business at hand. To help slay Stella, the Dragon and any bastard of an Ogre that got in his way.

We began to climb the sheer cliff of Dover in the wilderness of the unknown, and my body shook inside with each treacherous foot and hand hold we took. The rope was secure about my waist, and Hemsley was my total security as well as my life line to safety.

I knew that his strength would carry me through all the dangers that stood in our way, and as we kept a slow and steady pace. My fears slowly subsided and my fear of height would soon end right here upon this dangerous mountain that lead the way to the dragon's lair high above where we paused for a breath of crisp fresh air.

In our midst was a small cavern that had placed itself right square in our path as if some magical spell had came down from my Mother Earth and the great Mother of all Goddess' Shauna of Davenport who hailed from our town of Alexander in my Angleland.

Drawing his water pelt, William gave me the first drink of water from it, and it sure did quench my thirst from all the dust that had collected from outside of this outlandish and harsh place we called the eastern sector.

The two bruit men Clancy and Hemsley had guzzled most of their water down their gullets like it was nothing. Water drizzled down their unshaven faces and splashed on their cloaks, but William took his time so not to spill one precious drop of our liquid substance, because he as well as I knew that we would need further down the line.

As we sat there resting our soaked and weary bodies, I felt something nudge my butt from behind me; quickly I jumped up and screamed as I looked at one of the most hideous creatures that I had ever seen in my life. It was a green Ogre jelly; a slimy substance that was about half a foot wide and some ten foot in length and only preys on flesh. If it had taken hold of me before I moved I might have been digested in its acid. It would have wrapped itself about my body and squeezed until all of my bones were broken and made into ashes so it could consume even their contents. I t would have been a horrible death, but I thank the great spirits for protecting me through the use of my dear William and his companions.

"Step aside Princess and we shall slay this horrid creature." William was the first to draw his sword, then Clancy, and Sir Hemsley drew his bow and arrows as fast as he could and shot into the slimy creatures jelly like mass. William and Clancy sliced it into pools of goop that shivered like lime green jelly that slowly started to meltdown into a liquid form and penetrate back into the ground of the cavern whence it had emerged.

I breathed heavily and held my mouth closed as tight as I could so that I wouldn't inhale the acidic fumes. William and the others popped their heads out of the cavern entry to get a fresh breath of air and I followed their lead to sooth my throat from the acidic odor as well.

"Thank you all, you saved my life. How can I ever repay you for your courage?" I continued to cough from my sudden panic attack of acid reflux and foul tasting odors that slightly penetrated my nostrils and lingered to my throat. I spat a few times, but didn't care how unbecoming it looked to the men, because it was a necessity as well as to pick the gooey slime from my nose with several of my finger tips.

"You are always at our service Princess Yvonne." Both Sir Hemsley and Sir Clancy stated at the same exact moment, and my William Dear bowed gracefully to my presence; telling me his... your welcome also.

I was relieved and somewhat nicer to Hemsley, Clancy and my beloved William for their noble deed of helping save my life.

We climbed back out onto the sharp jagged spears of golden Bloodstones and malachite and eased our way onward and upward for what seemed to be another hour or so as the sun slowly set to our westward region.

Finally we reached our destination someplace near the dragon's lair, and the view was spectacular as we looked out over the terrain far and wide. I glanced down and took a slight dizzy spell and almost fell off the cliff, but Clancy grabbed a hold of my ass and pulled me back a couple feet so I wouldn't be killed, because he now realized how dangerous our quest really was and knew that if I were to be killed here on this mountain, that all of the rest of them and our village would all die eventually from the Black Dragon and my evil step-sister Stella Davenport toe cruel witch of the east.

"Careful Princess, you do not want to fall now doest thee." Clancy's old English and Scottish voice seemed a little gentler for some reason. Maybe he was changing for the better now that he realized his purpose at last; well at least I hoped so any way.

I began to hum a tune that harmonized with my surroundings and I heard intervals of musical instruments playing in my mind's eye; it had a moodiness of medieval quality and a prevailing dominatrix sensitivity, and I wished that I had my black boars leather outfit and whip so I could tame both Clancy and Hemsley as I had done to my dear William the guardian of Welsh who be mine Prince Charming and future King and mīn (my) only true lufian (love).

There was a subtle relationship aimed toward the east as my humming became somewhat louder in pitch, but I didn't know the consequences of what was about to befall upon me and my travel companions.

In the distant wind came an echo to my purring, but much deeper in tone and as it came closer it got worse in pitch; like a giant bull calling out in-order to draw female cows to its side so it could breed with them one by one till it was satisfied that it had enough sex for one day.

As we all looked toward the north, we saw a huge Ogre that stood nearly nine or ten feet tall and it must have weighed in the neighborhood of six or seven hundred pounds or so. God it sure was an ugly man like beast of a creature. I must have lured it from its cavern with my musical notes, but how was this possible; Ogre usually hide in wait so they can attack trespassers that came into their territory?

We quickly hid behind one of a couple hundred boulders near the color-ad-o river that flowed toward the east and disappeared down the mountainside making several beautiful waterfalls that I sure did long to shed my rags and take a nice long cold bath beneath its refreshing mounds of water in pools far below the cliffs of jagged danger to our west.

My evil step sister sure did pick a beautiful as well as dangerous place to reside, and once she was gone, them I would claim this land for my very own as well as what I already had in my possession.

As we glared up at the monster that stood in front of the boulders it gave off a repellent odor that to them was natural, but repulsive to us humans. Its skin color was a toss up between a dull brown and a dull yellow, and its clothing just as repulsive as it was; it wore cured furs and hides that were in poor condition, and filled with dust, dirt and acidic urine like odors. Most ogres had overwhelming odds of sneak attacks and ambushes most of the time, but this one was one of the most stupid creatures I could ever imagine in my mind's eye.

It would not fight fairly if we confronted it, so we decided to stay low so it couldn't see us, or it would attack us immediately without any questions, but if we would have walked into its path, it would speak Giant in its usual common and boastful mannerism as most Ogre do in this land of unreal thoughts that we hide in.

Now if this was a band of Ogre we would be in really big trouble because when they are in gangs they fight like unorganized individuals against their foes, and their weapons of choice are big redwood trees that they carve into crude clubs with bumps and points protruding from the huge ball at the end of their tangled leather animal and sometimes human skin handle grasps.

"Me have go; me find no where go; me will have go mess here in open me think." The Ogre untied its furry hide from its waist and squatted down like a woman going to the bathroom right in front of us. It was a horrible sight to behold, and the smell that it let out from its ass was worse than one of our sewers. In about four or five minutes it had finished its duty and tied the furry hide back around its waist, looked down at what it left behind it and went on its way. As soon as it left our sight, we ran as far away from where the Ogre left its mess so we wouldn't smell it any longer.

"Ogre are nasty beast my princess, are they not my Princess." William said as he continued to hold his nose from the disgusting smell that the Ogre filled the air with.

"Yes, yes Sir William, they sure are nasty and grotesque. What would have happened if it would have seen us may I ask." I too held my nose, but looked away toward the east and not directly Hemsley, Clancy or my handsome and soon to be King of Kings; Sir William.

"My princess, we would have had to kill it, that is all there is to it my lady." Clancy took a breath of air as he told me what he would have done to the giant half man half beast of a creature that didn't have one single brain in its big fat ugly skull.

"That is right Princess Yvonne, I and my friends here would have had to slay it and cut off its head to give warning to the other beast that this would be their fate too if they were to confront us." William was bold with his words, and that made me feel even more secure than I had been.

"I will be relieved when we finish our quest, slay the Black Dragon, and destroy my evil step-sister Stella, that devils daughter who had brought shame upon myself and my family. I will make her pay with her very own life and hope she burns in her own iniquities. She will deserve everything that we all dish out to her in return for all that she has done to us and our people." I stood stronger than I had been.

As time went by, my strength grew bigger than any Ogre ever would obtain; this was one thing for certain that I started to notice about myself which no one else noticed until now. William saw right through me, but he loved me more than I loved him for some reason at this particular moment.

It was necessary for me to try and act like an adult now more than ever before; even though I was only a sixteen year old girl, or so I thought, but sometimes it was essential in order to get my way as most teenagers so often do when they are all stressed out, or locked up inside themselves with only selfishness.

I knew my needs and wishes were more important than those of other people, and I had to do what I had to do in order to keep my word to not only myself, but to my people as well.

I began to look deep inside my subconscious at these desires, and they outweighed my immediate needs which couldn't be helped at this time of fear and anxiety; because of my personal goals to have William as my husband and be by my side in the castle Davenport to help rule my kingdom, but what was more important at this time was to achieve our objective and make our way to the lair of Stella and the demon black dragon and end their lives, take the blood from the fire breathing beast and then head home to cure the diseased people of Alexandria.

In my mind I sometimes had a great deal of confusion when there was more than one criteria as well as crisis to overcome in such a short period of time in such a horrid land filled with mush uncertainty.

My powers were not quite as strong as I would like them to be, but when I did finally destroy my step-sister and have the dragon slain, and take its blood so I can cure our people of the Black Plague; then and only then would my powers be at full strength and nothing could stop me from gaining more wealth, more land and more power than anyone could ever imagine in their mind's eye; not even my dear William whom I loved deeply.

There were many women in Alexandria that had no man because death fell on their heads, and they would jump at the chance to stealest a man like Sir William the guardian of Welsh away from me if they knew just how good of a lover he really was, and I surely am not about to blab my mouth to any of those ugly mongrel female bitches; most of which are of a mixed-breed, especially the ill-natured or worthless ones. They are not any type of mongrel dog nor mixed-breed of a she cur, especially ill-natured or worthless ones. They are not any kind of contemptible person for any man let alone a good man like he is. I consider them retched, cowardly, or otherwise unpleasant to even look at let alone make love with.

Here in this uncharted land there appears to be so many dangers and this even confuses me as to if I really want this place as part of my kingdom, but if by great chance we can get rid of all of these monstrous creatures, then I would have more than any other kingdom on Mother Earth, and I would be the most powerful of any witch that bore the title of witch.

"Princess, we will be at the lair of the dragon in another three or so days from now, and it is my opinion that we should make shelter as soon as we can find a safe enough place that don't have any monsters like these that we have encountered thus far in our journey." William was calm and collective like a cucumber ready to be placed in a salad; speaking of which, I was getting mighty hungry and wondered what we were going to eat as we traveled.

Some how I had forgotten that our previsions were tied to big ugly Clancy's back because he was the strongest of us all and could bear the weight with ease.

"I am hungry, but may I ask prey-tell what am I to eat?" My stomach growled like a hungry wolf as I held it lightly with my left hand and held onto William's arm with my right.

"Clancy is carrying our food Princess, or have you forgotten." William charged with his sudden ill mannerism, but gentle tone of voice.

I started to get angry once again, but couldn't bring myself to explode in their faces if I was to achieve my ultimate goal. "I-I, I did forget for just a brief moment; why yes my brave man; my... (I almost said my lufian (love), but caught myself) Sir William, you are totally right? Come on now lets sit a spell right here and eat before I melt away like that slime done back there in the cavern." I plopped myself down on a near by fallen Ash tree and waited patiently for Clancy to take off the food pack from his back and distribute portions of dry roasted goat meat, goat cheese, herbal corn bread and palm wine. My mouth watered so.

I ate till I was ready to burst wide open from my backside like the Ogre had done, and I had to find a place so I could go and not be seen by my three male traveling companions, that would really embarrass me to the point of having to turn around and go back to Alexandria a defeated princess and a failure as a woman to my dear William.

I didn't know why this feeling came over me all of the sudden, but it did? Maybe it was from what I had just eaten or maybe it was some sort of spell that my evil step-sister had placed on me so I would give up and turn back, but I wasn't about to let even this stand in my way of success. I had to go and that was that.

"I must command privacy for a short time, so you all will just have to go ahead for a short distance so I can do what I have to do." I looked at them with pain in my eyes and held my bowels as best I could so I wouldn't smell like a disgusting Ogre or foul smelling beast like a skunk or even a mele with a digestive problem.

They headed off for a short distance and I went quickly behind the log and squatted and let loose with such force that I couldn't even stand my own smell, but nothing would ever top that of the Ogre.

The secretes of my digestive tract had an acidic odor and would soon dissolve any organic matter that came in contact with it as it plunged to the ground beneath my feet. I shuffled my feet several times to move forward away from the mess as quickly as I could, but it kept coming like water flowing from one of the many water falls to the sough of me. To make matters worse for me, I shuffled myself out away from behind the log just enough to cause all three men to look back in my direction for a brief moment, but they turned around hoping that I didn't notice them looking at me from the distance. It was embarrassing, but all I could do was to try and ignore the whole incident except for the smell that effected my breathing and sinuses, but it wasn't effecting the stones, but it did make the tree branches from the log dissolve and shrivel as if a melee had taken hold of them with its constricting attack, causing much acid damage to the once green leaves of its stems that protruded from the logs shaft.

I soon finished what I had to do, and pulled up my dress rags as fast as I could and ran to where my companions were standing and cackling away like a small pack of old hens.

As I approached them, I heard Hemsley say to them. "I bet the smell was atrocious like that of the Ogre." He laughed as did the William and Clancy.

"How dare you speak in such a manner like that about me your Princess?" I threw my anger at them, but gave way to a different tune almost immediately and laughed right along with them and said. "I am relieved to see you are all in good spirits, and yes it was an unpleasant odor." I continued to laugh, but kept my anger tied up inside like a wounded animal laying in its den or burrow.

Almost everything I did raised eyebrows from my three brave warriors, and regrettably I could not do very much in secret, but openly so all could view my dark, musty occult side of life that I have dwelling inside of me. I think that I am a sincere and devoted witch to my deity and to my great mother and father rest their souls and it deeply implanted in my roots of all of humanity that I must draw on that benefit of both humanity and my Mother Earth herself.

It is not so profoundly put that my somewhat evil witch's ways are also of a different breed like that of my evil step-sister Stella who calls herself a Satanist or a devil-worshiping witch. My ways lean toward good and I so much want to make change to my ways of witchcraft and worship, because I am drawn apart at the seams at times and not knowing what way to really turn when faced with pressure, and being made fun of by those who would not respect my Goddess and Princess' powers.

I could destroy all that make me to be a fool and poke fun at me the way they have, just because I am a young girl and not at my full maturity yet, but I won't because I do care about them just a little bit.

Surely there must be a whole lot more witchcraft circles than mine on this planet I call Mother Earth, but why are they not joined with me to do my bid and make way for a better life than this impoverished and beastly realm. Is this place worth trying to take control of, or should I let it be as it is after I get rid of Stella and her pet the Black Dragon.

My confusion flowed through my mind's eye like the rivers below me and the ocean to my west, it towers high like these Bloodstone and golden malachite cliffs all the way to my Father Sky, and I must be like a snap-dragon and come out of my wondering thoughts before I break down and wilt like the branches from the ash tree where I lay my waste a couple miles behind me for some dumb Ogre to step its big foot in; that would be funny and I laughed aloud.

"Hahahahahaha." A big smile came over my face and my outburst of sudden laughter caught my companion's ears and forced them to glair at me like the hot and unwanted suns beating rays.

"Are you alright my Princess? Is the sun and heat getting to ya just a wee bit now lass." Clancy was performing his usual rhetoric by using his other accent that he used from time to time just because he was of Scottish descent as well as being from Anglelish descent. His mother was from my country, but his father was from Scotland where they have fierce and brave warriors amongst their people, but here in Angleland we have few brave souls to do our bid in times of desperation like this quest we were on.

"I am alright sir!" I exclaimed and kept on walking like it was nothing.

Keeping up with the three big men wasn't easy for me, and even worse was their crude and rude remarks, but I had to put up with their crap, or get left behind and not be able to use my powers when the time came to use them. I was not about to be left in this Goddess forsaken land of misery and death that knocks at every open door of opportunity that it has when presented with its invitation to enter there- in, and kill anything in its way of total freedom to do as it will.

My mind is strong willed, but childish at the same time, and now I know it was time to be a mature adult, a true Goddess among witch princesses and show some backbone and leadership skills to these things that are called men. Ha, I thought, I will show these men that I am as brave and strong as they are, just you wait and see. I will, yes me truly will that is for certain.

Chapter 4
Battle for the Ogres Cave

Night fall was almost upon us and the dusk was on its way before our eyes. It would be more dangerous at night than in the daylight, and we needed shelter as fast as we could find it.

As we turned towards the southern edge of a short canyon, we saw a series of big caves all in a row as if giants had carved then out with their monstrous blows from their redwood clubs.

We all knew it was the work of a band of Ogre, but what kind of Ogre were they, the dumb kind like the one who dropped its fur hide in front of my eyes and left its awful smelly mess in our path, or was it the intelligent kind that used small spell powers to defeat its foes. All I knew was I needed sleep as did my brave companions and to just walk into one of those caves and confront what ever was inside would possibly mean our deaths.

We knelt down behind some small boulders that had been stacked to one side as if they were used in catapults of some sort for war battles. Clancy knew that we would have to fight and fight hard to win one of these caves in order to get a half way descent nights sleep.

He had a plan to draw out the Ogre, but it would not be an easy task. We first had to get their attention by making one of us a decoy and luring them away from their caves far enough and in a direction that they would be lost for a couple days trying to find their way back to their cozy cave homes in the misty mountains of the eastern sector that was now two days journey from our port of entry into the dragons lair.

Clancy gathered three blades of snake grass, and pulled a piece off one of them so who ever drew the short one would have to be the decoy while the others took possession of the cave, and then once out of sight of the Ogre could come back and join the rest of us.

I looked as he picked only three and I did not want to be left out of this part of our journey so I pulled another blade and gave it to him.

"I am a part of this too you know, and you are not going to leave me out for any reason." I looked at all three of them with mean eyes and they knew I meant business or else I would have them all punished once we returned to our town.

"Princess Yvonne; if you do this will you be able to out do the Ogre and evade them as well as to make your way back here to join the rest of us." William said as he knew what I was capable of when I put my mind to it, so we proceeded to pick straws.

I did not know that Sir Clancy, Sir Hemsley and my Dear Sir William had planned it so that I would be the one who was the decoy, because I was the smallest, smartest and fastest of all of us and would be out of the way when the real fighting started. They knew that not all of the Ogre would leave their caves because they had to protect their families like anything else on earth do when confronted with an enemy.

"I have drawn the short one and will join you back here as soon as I can, so pray that I escape these beastly Ogres safely so we can complete our quest for the dragon's blood and cure our people once and for all and end all of these curses that have befallen on us." I bid them farewell and wondered out into the open like a fool, but at least I would be a brave fool as well as a brave Princess if I didn't get myself killed in the whole damned process just to get a good nights sleep in a mean old Ogre cave.

"Be careful my princess, they have a deadly blow force behind their powerful arms, and if one of the clubs would hit you in such a way, then you might die, or be lame for eternity, that is if you escaped such a blow from the Ogres club." William told me with concern in his beautiful eyes.

"Look behind your back constantly Lass whilst you run and hide in different spots, you are small enough to hide almost any place, and also you must keep your eyes open for the smooze creatures, they could be any place and they do kill almost instantly on contact with ones flesh." Hemsley said with much concern as well.

They all knew I would do good enough to lure the ghastly beasts far-far away to the point of almost no return.

54

I shouted toward the cave as loud as I could. "I am lost is there anyone inside one of these caves? I need a place to stay because it is getting dark and I am afraid."

Before I finished shouting, the earth beneath my feet shook as if I was in an earthquake, but it was the thunderous thumping of their weight that brought them scurrying outside toward me?

They were ghastly monsters; and must have been about twelve of them, they were all well over ten feet tall and more than seven or eight hundred pounds in mass. The smell was even bad at such a distance as I was away from them and I didn't know if at that point that I wanted to sleep in one of their gas filled and poopy caves or not let alone be in this danger that I and the others had placed me into.

The Ogre looked at me and me at them, and then I took off like a speeding steda in a foot race across the treacherous terrain toward the south and the water falls. I too had my own plan to lure them over the edge of the cliff and into the rocky filled bottom of a huge waterfall to their death. Where one went the others followed as I ran to and fro between boulders, trees and mounds of Mojave Desert sand that had been transported here many millennium ago by my ancient ancestors to help beautify this land, but it had been placed in the wrong place and not our beloved land near my castle Davenport.

It was hard for them to hit me because I was almost as fast as the lightening that my Father Sky sent down to Mother Earth once in awhile just to wake her up sometimes for the spite if things and have a little fun with her and making her to ruffle her feathers a wee bit now and then.

Swoosh went their clubs, one right after the other, as they took swings at my small body; and sometimes they would accidentally hit one another causing a fight would break out amongst two of them and then they would tromp as fast as their big size twenty feet would make them run just to catch up to their band of stinky and somewhat clumsy breed of beast family and not so close friends.

I could not help but to laugh at them from time to time and that made them even madder than they already were at me.

One big ugly Ogre told the others that he would pin me next to the cliff where a giant waterfall streamed down to a rocky and watery grave below.

"Claude go trap human, and then ya come to sees it; keep selves here till Claude calls ya." His tone was rough and large as he ran toward me with his big club raised high above his head. I immediately had a plan to get rid of all of the Ogre at one time, since there was a waterfall next to where I was standing to catch my breath, I just stood there waiting for it to come as close as he could then I would make the others mad enough to come running at their friend so I could escape.

"Claude gonna git ya; yous mine hahahahaha." His huge body pounded the ground with thunder and it shook like an earthquake, but I stood my ground ad the beast came upon me at the edge of the cliff by the waterfall.

"Beast, you will never take me alive; you are ugly and smelly like all of your ugly friends." I yelled at it with a fierce cry as it stood over me with its club ready to pound me into the ground, but I was small enough to look between its legs and see the others waiting to run and join him.

He glared at me with squinted hairy eyes and its tongue hung out like a rabid dog in heat. Dwell ran down its face and sweat dripped from its half covered body as I stood beneath its shadow. Some of the slimy goo dripped down from its blackened tongue and hit me on the head; I swiped at it with a fury trying to wipe it off of me, but couldn't because I had to concentrate on the beast that stood in front of me. The slobber smelled worse than the Ogre itself and I wanted to just turn and dive into the waterfall myself, but knew if I did that, then I would die, and not see William, his friends and our town, nor would I be able to rid my people of the Black plague and my evil step sister and her pet the Black Dragon.

I called to the other beasts to bring them to where I was as fast as their fat ugly selves could bring them.

"You are the smelliest and ugliest things ever created, come and get me if you have the insides enough to take me." I shouted as loud as I possibly could and it got their attention.

The one who called itself Claude turned around to yell at then to stay put for a second and I hit jumped on its big foot making him look back down at me, but it was too late the others were almost upon us with a thunderous roar of the ground shaking beneath my feet. I had the beast in such a position to escape then all at last.

A few seconds later they were next to us and breathing heavily with more slobber dripping down their faces and the smell almost made me through up. One of the other dumb Ogres took a swing as it approached the pack and it missed me and almost hit Claude on his foot.

I ran between Claude's legs and as I did I looked up, yuk, the horrible thing that hung down between its legs made me gag a little and I spat on its foot as I stood behind them and glanced at the last one who was a little slow catching up to the others. It was swinging its club back and forth like a mad person, well beast and as it came close enough it hit another one in the face causing it to stumble into the others and fall over the edge of the cliff to a watery and rocky grave below.

The force of its swing also had enough force to plunge it over the edge along with the others. I stood their looking over the ledge as they all fell shouting and swing at each other like a crazy grizzly bear who wanted to tear its extended family apart with sharp claws, but it was the Ogre's clubs doing the swinging and not a mean mad bear.

Splish splash- they all went they all went one after the other into the jagged and churning water below the falls. I was relieved that I had killed a dozen Ogre with just one glancing blow, and now I could go back to where the my companions were fighting the remaining beast that had stayed behind to protect their caves from us humans.

As I walked I wiped some of the slobber from my head and face onto my dress the best I could, but even that made me stink worse than I already was, and knew I would have to go beneath one of the other waterfalls to clean myself up as soon as I could.

I also thought of another spell to make my Dear William safe, and make his heart one with mine for eternity.

Back at the cave the others were in a battle for their lives as well.

Clancy took a swing at one of the Ogre and hit it in the chest with his sword and it screams from the small cut he had made after it tore its fur hide making it even madder than it was. There were four against three, but not as great as odds as I had when I was fighting my Ogre's back at the waterfall. Little did I or my companions know that the Ogre I forced over the waterfall never really perished; but swam to the Acsan múða (the mouth of the river) where they lay under the sun and in the midst of hundreds of big tall áctréos (oak-trees?)

William took a swipe at different one and cut its hand off making it run like the wounded animal it was, blood oozed from it as it ran and splashed all over the place, a few minutes later it fell upon the cold hard ground in front of its cave, little did any of us know it too didn't die, because Ogre live for ever, and their wounds heal themselves in just a matter of hours.

One down and three more to go, Hemsley got hit by one of our foe and fell hard to the ground with the beast hovering over him ready to pound him into the ground with its club, but Clancy took his bow and arrow and shot a couple arrows into it. One hit it in the leg and made him scream, another lunged into its throat and blood pumped out like a water hose on a raging fire. It fell to the ground and almost landed on William, but he rolled out of the way just in the nick of time and the mighty ugly beast lay beside him as if it were a dead stump as well. Some of its green blood flew on William and even it smelled foul ad he lay their shaking his head, the other two were on top of Hemsley and Clancy.

William got up as fast as he could and ran toward them with his sword swinging fast and furiously at his approach he swiped at the head of one and cut off its eat, another swipe cut into its neck, Hemsley swung at its neck as well and made enough contact to cut its head the rest of the way off and fall to the ground and roll away as its body plunged to the ground behind it and flopped around like a fish out of water and died.

That left one more who tried to escape, but Clancy, Hemsley and William shot arrows into its back and thought they had killed the last remaining Ogre by the caves and the battle was over.

Clancy had suffered a badly bruised shoulder and it began to swell slightly, William ended up with a big headache from the blow he suffered from one of the Ogre's clubs, and Hemsley had a few cuts and scratches on his arm, face and legs from the sharp edges of his opponents clubs, but all in all they were all alive, safe at last and very tired.

Meanwhile I was on my way back and had cast my Two Hearts as One spell upon my wonderfully brave prince charming Sir William, and we were as one in thought and spirit.

I finally arrived back to the caves where William was waiting outside. Hemsley and Clancy were inside and had started a fire for warmth. They had found a huge boulder that had been carved into some kind of bathing tub of sort and had stripped down to nothing and were bathing together in it. As we started walking inside, they were kissing each other with lots of deep passion, none like my little dark eyes had ever seen the likes of before; I covered my eyes when I saw their hairy naked bodies and them bathing each other like a couple of crazy and YUCKY sick in the head disgusting ill mannered and gai (gay)- lesbian; hine/hēo (he/she) sorta half-assed men if one could call this breed such things as human men let alone brave men, but I had to at least give them the benefit of doubt as to their bravery. To me that was more disgusting than seeing the Ogres ugly private parts when I was battling it, and I buried my head in Williams chest and he lead me back outside where we sat holding each other for about another hour and then we went back inside the cave to join our two gay companions, but we never said a single word as to us seeing them engaged in semi-sexual activity.

"Yewwwwww; how horrid; what mannerism be this now, YUCK how GROSS." I hid my face in William's big chest so hard it almost cut off the oxygen to my brain.

"Princess, I-I... I am sorry that you and Sir William has seen that which we are engaged in; yes tis true me lady... please Princess do not think any bad of us... for we are in love." Clancy said with much embarrassment and indecent humility to his heightened blushful face.

"I L-ass, my Princess tis indeed true, we be in love, that we be." He too was blushing like a little school girl that had her cloak torn away from her exposing her small but meek bosoms to her class mates.

"William, let us go and leave these two alone and maybe we should leave them here on this horrid mountain top for the beasts to devour." I too was embarrassed to the Outer Limits of My Young Mind's Eye, but had not much choice but to just shut up and put up with this ill mannerism of what I thought were two men; yuck was my only thought as we walked away from the disgustingly foul and lustful sins that these two half-assed men were doing to each other.

It was a shameful thing to see, Yuk, two grown men bathing each other all over and laughing about it. That is one thing that I shall never forget as long as I am alive here upon my Mother Earth. How sick can some people be I thought as I talked to William discussing our total day's strenuous activities and fierce battles including the gay sight that we'd made witness to a short time back?

"Good fighting, ahhhumm... men, well done. I shall reward you all greatly upon our return home, but for now we must try to get our rest so we can continue our quest for the dragon's blood in the morning." I stood firm, my arms were on my hips with authority as I walked toward William who was standing beside a pile of freshly taken furs that had not been laid to dry and cure in the sun's mighty rays as they should have been, but after all this was an Ogre's cave and what more could one expect from such filthy and disgusting beasts; not only the Ogre, but Clancy and Hemsley as well.

William and I lay down together and our companions didn't say a single word but went off to a more secluded and somewhat darkened part of the cave and out of our sight.

"William." I said with a half way smile on my tired lips. Do you think our companions, Sir Clancy and Sir uhhhhhhuuuummmmm, Hemsley are just a little strange in their behavior. I do not know what kind of men, uhhhhhuuummmmm half men they really are? I thought they were men, but their actions here tonight show me uhhhuuummmmm otherwise." I could not help but gag and clear my throat at the very thought of such filthy and disgusting behavior as they displayed and right before my young and innocent eyes.; how disgusting… yuck, just the sheer thought almost made me vomit like a dirty, filthy, mangy cur bitch of a dog.

I sure was beat to a pulp and soon fell fast asleep on the bed of furs that lay against a back wall of the damp and dreary cave that once had belonged to the Ogre and now ours as long as we wanted them for.

Chapter 5
Stella's Evil that Hinder the Way

Morning came faster than I hoped it would, but that was alright too, because I wanted to get on with my quest no matter what object, monster, or human flesh eating creature confronted us or got in my way. I knew that I and my men, well at least one of them was a man, the other two, I just was not sure if they were men or what, but even they were ready to do battle and overcome obstacles no matter what was said or done.

"Wake up you lazy grunts, oh and you too Princess Yvonne." Clancy said with his usual Oscar the grouch voice. "Come on now, let's get a move on; we have a ways ta go before we reach da top of this mountain and the lair of the dragon." He raised his red eyebrows and half-ass smiled at Sir William hoping that we had not noticed what he and Hemsley had done the night before.

"Aaaaahhhhh ummm; huh, yes we best be moving before more Ogre show up." William said as he slowly woke up from a sound sleep.

Hemsley seemed more tired than Clancy for some reason, but I was not about to ask him why and if he/she was alright or not.

The smell of dead Ogre's were all about us and I almost threw up as I popped my head outside in the bright early morning eastern sunrise and looked at the smelly beasts bodies hewn haphazardly all over the place in random spots.

The Ogre was only tired and just wanted to sleep until the sun was high in the Eastern Sky above them.

As we walked a short distance around a slight bend in what looked like another canyon we came upon still another sheer cliff standing in our faces.

"Damned the luck." I shouted. "What the hell kind of place is this with blocked passage ways of steep jagged and sharp gold toned malachite and Bloodstone cliffs hewn to and fro as though placed here on purpose." I said with a slight angry growl in my squeaky pitched voice. Somehow I knew it must have been the workings of my evil step-sister Stella some time during the past several years of living here in the eastern sector. Surely our creator would not make such an awful place as this here upon the Great Mother Earth with Father Sky looking onward at it being made; surely he would have said something to our creator about why he made this living hell? I had many such questions in my mind, and it frustrated me so, but what could I do about it when I am so desperate to finish this whole matter so I can get on with my life as a married woman, and Goddess of my kingdom no matter what it took.

"Would ya look here now, we have still another cliff to climb, but this time we will not stop until we reach da top, so lets get a move lads and you too my pretty lil' lass." Clancy was the one who most of the time open up his big mouth of a trap first and gave us the orders instead of me and I let him for some strange reason, but did not know why to this important question either.

"Time stands still for no one; I guess if we must climb still another one, we best get it done and over with, ahhhhhhh; Sir Clancy I am not your lass and never shall be is that clear my good uhmmummm man" I sighed just slightly, with a ho hum and a disgusting ill mannered glance into the eyes of the mixed up- messed up gay he/she Clancy; or was it because I was sluggish and somewhat bored from the lack of oxygen that was getting to my still tired brain; I did not know and was more than ready to give up altogether and go home by myself, but before I had a chance to say another word; William tied the rope about my waist once again and picked me up with both of his strong arms by my tiny butt placing me atop a small flat top boulder with several sword like edges sticking up beside it. They were like sharp fangs sticking out of the mouth of a snake and we had what looked like millions of them to contend with in this climb as well.

The wind began to blow as I reached up for a safer surface as William hands lifted me up once again, I felt one finger touch my mid section bringing back the memories of his love making to me, but I had to shake the feeling out of my head. Hemsley pulled himself up onto the first ledge behind me and then shimmed himself to one above me so he would be able to lift me with his rāp as William helped me from my behind.

I did not like Hemsley touching my ass in front of others, but what could I say or do about it. I guess not a damned thing, and I just did not give a damn either, because I knew he would not want me in a sexual way because of his strange and gay behavior with Sir Clancy in the cave last night. I knew I was in good safe hands even under the circumstances of being with one real man and two things that called themselves men.

Up-up-up we went as the wind blew stronger by each ridge we reached, and it became harder and harder as we went along our un-enjoyable way. It seemed to be getting colder, the higher we climbed and my hands began to tingle with the chill of the air and that made it even harder still to get hand holds. Once in awhile the cold wind blew up my dress and made my legs and other parts shiver with millions of goose-bumps all over them. I knew I needed rest as did the others, but this time there was not any cavern or crevasse to climb into and take a break.

I looked up and we still had about another hundred or so feet to go until reaching the top of this thorny cliff and then we could rest for a short time before we would be able to eat again.

For some out of the ordinary reason, and I did not know why; I was hungry more than I usually was. My stomach kept growling at me like a lone wolf ready to chew me apart if I upset it any more than it already was. Maybe it was from the altitude that we were in that made me hungry, I did not understand what my body was trying to tell me, but it sure was something that was for certain.

"We are almost their Princess Yvonne. AHHHHHH AHHHHHH." William's breathing was heavier than when he had made love to me a couple weeks ago back in Alexandria in his hut. I looked up at him with my bedroom eyes and ask him if he was alright.

"I am; my Prin-cess Y-vonne, I am alright. I am on top now, come on my love give me your hand so I can pull you over the ledge to the top." I reached my hand up toward his and looked at Clancy who had one hand on my ass. I gave him a dirty glare to get his weird hands off of me and told him I could make it by myself now. He pulled his hand away as soon as I told him to.

"Yes, ahahahahhh my Prince-ss." His face was all sweaty and he was shivering from the chilly air that brushed against the side of the cliff. I looked at my dear William and he too was almost frozen from the glacial air.

Finally we were on top, but it started to warm just a tad on the top, only on the side was the air colder, and I knew it was the workings of a chill spell that my evil step-sister had cast upon us to try and keep us away. How she knew we were headed her way was a mystery to me, but she knew, and I would soon find out how she was casting spells at us when she could not see that we were close to her dragons lair and long time home atop the eastern mountains.

Our breathing was heavy and the chills slowly subsided, leaving us warmed once again from the mighty sun's rays.

"Warmth at last, but I am still going to make us a fire to take the rest of the chill away from our cold and weary bones." Once again it was Clancy who spoke up first before I had a chance to say a single word, and this was getting me more aggravated than any monster or beast ever could get, and when the right time came I was going to make him stop giving me- his princess orders the way he was once and for all.

Hemsley got off his lazy butt and went to gather some dry ash and hemlock branches so big mouth Clancy could make a fire. I sat there and just starred at the both of them in anger, and my dear William noticed how mad I was really getting at them especially at big ugly and gay Clancy the male prostitute for men. I had an icky feeling in their presence and it made me sick to my stomach, but not enough to throw up.

"Are you alright Princess Yvonne?" William leaned over and whispered in my ear as the to male lovers went off to gather wood for the fire leaving me and my love all alone for awhile as they did their own thing out of our sight.

I thought to myself, good riddance and then said it aloud.

"Good riddance." I smiled at William and him at me and then we gave one another a big wet and slobbery kiss.

I could still smell the foulness from the Ogre's slime it had dwelled all over me and wanted to bath so much.

"William my love, will we ever get back to Alexandria in one piece." I asked with a true seriousness.

"Yes Yvonne we will that I promise you my love." hē said with confidence in his smile. "Yes we most certainly will make it back alive because you and I are one in soul, heart and mind now my beautiful lass." Hē showed me his heart and it was one with mine, but he did not know that I had placed a two in one heart spell upon him right after the battle of the Ogre's.

The other two came back way sooner than we had hoped for and threw the wood down bedside us and began to fix it in a tower fashion on top of some rocks in a sandy area and lit it with the sparks from some flint stone that they had also gathered because it would come in handy later on as the day slowly passed by.

The fire took ablaze fast on the dried wood and would stay lit for hours and not turn to ashes like normal wood does in our world far below us. This wood seemed much healthier and a whole lot more stronger than that of our towns wooded areas, and I wanted to possess it along with everything else that I could get my greedy little hands on to make me the most powerful witch in the world of magic here on my ácennicge (mother) Earth.

This was my world and I wanted not just a small portion of it, but the whole thing and I was going to soon have what I set out to get, and that was revenge with my evil demonic witch of a step-sister Stella and her demon pet the Black Dragon of the east. They would very soon be dead and I could have a better life, my life once and for all at any cost and I did not care more than that at this particular time because I was getting tired from the long hard climb and wanted to eat a tiny bit of dried goat meat and lay down for a two hour nap before we continued our journey to still another plateau that would give me my much needed powers and a better way of life with my sweet and Dear William the Guardian of Welsh for eternity; providing we kept ourselves alive and as well as we have been doing this whole trip.

As we ate and warmed ourselves by Clancy's fire I could feel a storm brewing on the horizon, and it carried with it the price of destruction.

The winds picked up a bit more all of the sudden and the dust began to twist and twirl blowing in our faces. Harder and faster it twisted and blew, and the fire went out from the blowing dust and dirt. It had a force of a small tornado and an over powering ice storm at the same time. The sand was beating the piss right out of us all like a glass bead blaster at the forge where our swords were made. Its sting seemed to penetrate my arms and legs as well as my face and the pain it brought with it was the worse I had ever felt. There was no ice crystals in its midst, nor were there any other debris to fling itself against our bodies and it had a fiery heat to its content that was undesirable

I knew that in this land the weather pattern would change in a moments notice without any warning and could cause mass destruction when it was given the right conditions.

The next thing we knew it began to hail really hard from the tornadoes massive cloud high above us, and it too was beating the hell right out of us as if we hadn't already had enough of nature's weapons of mass destruction trying their best to kill us all.

I was madder than in pain, because I knew that everything that was happening to us was all the evil doings of that bitch of a witch Stella my awful step-sister.

I shouted at the top of my lungs.

"Stella- Stella, I will cyllan ēow (kill you) myself with my bare hands when we meet again you evil bitch; I will not give up and go home, never in a million life times will I quit. **I WILL CYLLAN ēOW (*KILL YOU*) THIS YOU CAN COUNT ON MY EVIL SISTER.**" I shouted at the tops of my lungs so my evil Bitch of a Half-Assed Step-Sister Stella could hear me; my anger was in a rage and I could not control it any longer and wanted to take off by myself as soon and as fast as I could so I could get to Stella as soon as I could and put her out of not only her misery, but out of my misery as well.

William grabbed a hold of me as tightly as he could so I wouldn't be blown away in the winds pounding, twisting and beating fury of hail and the fire stinging sands that the tornado picked up from our camp fire and was burning us with our own flames of power and heat.

"Princess, Hold on it will soon be over I can feel it letting up. Why did you shout the way you did, your sister will not hear you from this distance?" He too shouted in the might of the storm and in a moments notice, the tornado went as fast as it had come upon us.

"I have not felt such power before in my life. What on our Mother Earth was that my Princess." Sir Clancy said as he and Sir Hemsley the very first ever gays held onto each other so they would not be blown over the edge of the cliff that was almost beside our camp site.

They let go of one another and stood there in awe with their eyes popping out of their sockets like pop bottle rockets at one of our many festivals.

"That was a tornado my friends; have ge (you) not felt or seen one before?" William asked with an amazed and stunned look on his handsome unshaven face.

"Never in my life time have I felt such a powerful force of nature." Clancy said as he shook off the effects of the sudden twister's powerful storm of fury.

"Well you have now my funny friend, you have now… hahahahahaha." I could not help myself and had to laugh at the big ugly oaf and she-male. Yes that is what I shall call these kind of men who engage in sexual activity with one another, and if I were to see two women having sex with each other I shall call them she-she's or lesbians; and poke fun of them as much as I want and there would not be a thing they could do about it either because I will always be their ruler, Goddess and Princess of all princesses.

William laughed right along with me, but poor Clancy and Hemsley had no idea that we were laughing at them both instead of with þeim (them).

"You have not seen, nor felt anything yet. My step-sister Stella is a powerful witch, and she will use every trick in her book to render us useless and leave us for dead. Hēo (She) knows why wé are here and will try her best stop us from defeating her and her pet the Black Dragon if she possibly can." I looked at him with my head down slightly because of the embarrassment that he/ she or what ever it is and the other it, Sir, or might I say Madame Hemsley had put me and William through back at the Ogre caves was purely disgusting. Somehow I knew we did not have very far to go before we would make contact with my bitch-witch step-sister Stella and the beastly dragon who had caused harm on my people back home, but how she made it all happen I did not know, but knew I would find out how she caused the Black Death to destroy most of my loyal subjects.

After the tornado we walked a short distance behind stills another mountain, but this times it was just that a mountain and not a sheer cliff. It was a high mountain, and as I looked at it, my fear of height was completely gone from my whole earthly being. I sure was anxious to climb this one mostly without the help of anyone unless I really needed it, and then if I really did need help I would tell them I needed it.

I thought about Clancy giving most of the orders and that made me furious enough to tell him that I was in charge and not him and that he would follow my orders from here on out.

"Sir Clancy." I shouted. "I am your Princess am I not?" I asked with my demanding character.

"Yes you are my Princess." He replied.

"Well then Sir Clancy, who be in charge, I is that right?" I asked him with more of a demanding performance of attitude.

"Ummmm, yes my Princess?" He said with question in his ugly big mouth.

I replied to him with an even firmer character, and one with a strictness of a parent scolding their child. "Well then, I will give all of the orders from here on Sir Clancy…and not you; is that understood?" My eyes penetrated his as if they were dead eyes; and they were as black and as cold as a winter's night.

He looked puzzled and started to back talk to me, but I stopped him in his tracks with my fast tongue and quick intelligence.

"Do not dare talk back to me now or ever or I shall have you flogged when we get back to Alexandria; is that understood Sir, or shall I call you Madame instead?" I had to say it to him, and could not hold back any longer. It was hard for me to do, but I knew that I had to do what was necessary in order to show him and the others that I was totally in control of this quest as well as my kingdom.

Clancy sorta kept his big mouth closed like a clam that didn't want to be deep-fried any more.

We were almost to our destination and I prayed that we would not have any more setbacks the rest of the way to the top.

William told me that it should only take another day and maybe two at the most, but to me even that was not a short enough time span. My anxiety grew and made me a bit uneasy about this climb for some bewildering reason. After some of the things we had already been through what more beyond this could possibly go wrong. I had a great concern buried deep inside of my subconscious that made an unannounced appearance to my mind's eye.

Tremors filled my arms as the subconscious took control; I held much worry with a nervous twitch that almost turned into an agitation like a mysterious and powerful device for cleansing one's clothing of some type instead of the usual board that we used for this purpose.

I felt like something would go wrong and that because of my worries; something very serious was going to happen on this leg of our journey, but could not place my conscious thought patterns on it. The feeling was a little too strong at times causing more concern that was of the unnecessary kind.

It seemed to be an unhealthily strong feeling for me to do any one particular thing at any given time, and my legs froze like the Thames River in the dead of our artic chill season.

My wish became extremely apprehensive with an intensity of real fear, or was it my mind causing the immediate imagined danger and manifested physiologically increased heart rate, trembling, sweating, stomach discomfort, and weakness in my bones and flesh.

Suddenly I fell to the ground in limpness like a wet piece of pasta that was over cooked and sticky to the fingers when someone felt its posture. Min mind went blank all of the sudden and at a moments notice; William and the two eccentric and somewhat peculiarly strange men/ women or what ever they be; who are yucky lovers of sort rushed to my side to show their concern.

As they looked into my eyes, they saw only white and not pupil, because of the lack of blood flow and oxygen to my feminine brain that come upon a woman who was heavy with child in their early stage of bearing an baby; one might say I was bearnéacnigende (pregnant).

"I have seen this before." Said William with worry in his awkward and canny pitch.

"Yes and I too have seen it, but where?" Clancy looked totally confused and uncaring to a small fraction of his unconscious pea brain.

He too had a lack of oxygen all the time and was not even a little bit ill, well unless he/she was in the realm of psychopathic deliberation as to what to do next; with the exception of yucky Bedlam bed play of the non-reproductive union kind; YUCK, the conception of such a ghastly and nasty thing made me noxious and besides it was that of the devils wickedness, malice; a bit like saying it was a bealu act to say the least for it being baleful, deadly, dangerous, wicked, and an evil sin before the eyes of God and all who had the misfortune to have witnessed such a foul deed; **YUCK**… two grown men making love to each other; how sick can some people get. God have mercy upon your souls come judgment day.

As I lay there on the ground, I felt them placing their hands upon my brow and other body parts, but the chills out-weighed the strong palms and finger tips. I wanted to tell them; especially Clancy and Hemsley to just keep their filthy hands off of my body in the places that was allowed to be felt by no one except my dear wonderful sweet William only, but I could not say a word; my mouth was heavy and hanging down to my chin allowing a couple bugs to enter and then exit like a bees hive at their will. I heard their buzzing and the flapping of their tiny wings beating against their yellow and black bodies, and I could see not only my companions and what was their antic in my presence, but on the other side of the vision was the sight of the bugs themselves.

They were as giant bees that wanted to make sweet honey in their hive which was my open mouth at that time. It seemed impossible for such flying insect with a furry body that makes a buzzing sound as it flies to use my oral cavity as their honey factory.

Their stingers were like humungous black needles ready for a duel with my flesh or my companions flesh if they were bothered in their gathering for activity and friendly social competition. They seemed to be having not only social gathering, but work activities in combination to it.

The tang was sweet, and it left a nasty wild trace on my reddish, pink and partially black tongue with a coating of honey to sooth my want for bitter sweet bread and a cup of hot tea to accompany it. My stomach-churning was tangy… producing feelings of disgust, nausea, and fear; besides making hostile sounds, and communicated something to my brain by means of, a low nonverbal sound in the gullet, leaving a rotten egg sensation of dryness in my stoma (mouth) that expresses lack of sympathy towards my whole being that made me to snap out of a semi unconscious state of a near death experience.

As I struggled to set up with the help of William; I noticed that a portion of the top of my dress was untied exposing one breast and displaying its voluptuous beauty in the faces of those dirty old men.

"How dare you to expose my bearm (bosom) this way before these ugly things who call themselves men, how dare you Sir William." My anger along with my anxiety to achieve my goal to do in my step-sister Stella tool over control of my mouth and hindered me from using my brain to think before I spoke.

"Princess I needed to check your heart beat, and sees if you were breathing properly, after all you did faint just a short time ago. I thought you dead, but thank the Father Sky and Mother Earth you are alive." William made an apology in his own way and tried to smile at me as I re-tied my (dress) cloak to hide my lily white little breast once more and out of sight from sick and lustful minds of these men, well at least one man… I guess I should overlook the two Lesbian… he/she… uuuhhhmmmm sort of men.

"William my love what on Mother Earth just happen, I was fine, and then the last thing I knew; I was pulling myself up off the ground?" I tried to tell him I was also sorry for yelling at him the way I did, but could not bring myself to say I was sorry; instead I told him that if I was to pass out this way again with others around us that he was to take me behind something for more privacy and not show my wonderful flesh to any dirty old men like Clancy and Hemsley ever again.

He agreed as well as taking on a complete understanding of the word solitude and its meaning to be isolated when in the unconscious state of near death and receive the necessary help to breath properly with assistance from ones own lover and not beastly he/she creatures as Clancy and Hemsley as well as normal men and even women; well some are normal, but most are of the Neanderthal cave dwelling sorta bloke, and filthy cur she bitch dogs and the likes as unto a swine.

"This was an experience that I shall never forget as long as I live on my Mother Earth." I said as I looked at my Dear William the Guardian of Welsh with amazed eyes from the shock of being out of my conscience with the outlook of a sense of right or wrong; and the internal sense of that governs my every thought and alter ego of actions, urging someone to do right rather than wrong. It is obedience to my behavior in compliance with strictness and a shared concern for my moral issues as well as a concern of the social aspects of my superego that passes judgment upon those who do not deserve to be dealt a hand of foul language that is unbecoming from a lady and a princess such as me.

I thought to myself how rude I was and told myself that I would try my damnedest to do everything possible to show further consideration toward the man I love, but not to the others, because I was their superior and not they my commander and chief.

For some strange unheard of reason my now bluish like flesh crawled and had some bumps that itched me as though I had been powdered with some sort of solution like burning dust. Maybe it was this Mojave Desert dust that had been spread all over my body when the column of swirling wind from the tornados storm hit us awhile back.

So many things has happened to me over the past several days that I keep getting these flashbacks in memory that cause me to do and say things that I would not do in a millennium of centuries, even though I am only sixteen years of age.

My witchcraft powers were weak and maybe it was from the altitude and lack of oxygen or maybe it was because that witch bitch step-sister of mine Stella has placed bewitching spells on me causing me to falter enough so I can not use anything against her or her pet black dragon.

As we walked at a steady pace up the slopes of the mountain I could see its crest beyond a group of knotty ash trees and a thicket of hemlock that protruded their way from the bottom of still another cliff, but this one was not nearly as tall, nor sheer and as rugged as the other ones have been.

"I think my evil step-sister has forgotten to blaze this cliff with ridges of sharp fang like spears to hinder our way to the dragons lair and her home inside the caverns' of her beastly Neanderthal place of a volcanic cave of fire and brimstone." I stated to William and the other two weird estranged Fairy men who were accompanying us on our quest for blood and now my revenge to end Stella's life with a purple passion of insanity; and, I felt at times that I had became as a raving mad woman instead of a charming and proper lady of royalty and somehow my life had changed, but I did not know if it was for the best or worst that I could ever imagine.

I was happy that we be as close as we were as long as William stay near and dear to my heart, then I knew that all would turn out on the best side in no time at all.

Chapter 6
The Fatality of Clancy

There we were; right at the edge of where the beginning of the forest stood right in our faces; it was so thick that I did not think any of the swords would be able to cut their way through them. They had thorns all over their branches, not like the normal hemlock, because these were created from magic and not nature as all other spices of tree was created by the almighty Father Sky. These had properties of steal itself imbedded deep in their roots to make them the strongest substance that I had ever known of before.

"Ouch, these are sharp." I cried as I grabbed one to move its branch out of my way so I could walk through as I normally would, but they were way too strong for me to move. I wanted to ask William to move it out of my way, but instead I insisted that gay boy Clancy use his brute girly force against the thorny branch.

"I will be glad to be of service to you my Princess." Clancy outreached his strong arm and placed his big hairy handed fingers near the thorns and pushed with all his might and only moved it a centimeter or so before it went back in its stronghold place and remained steadfast.

"Let me try my dear sir. Stand aside my good man and I shall move this with my sword." Hemsley howled as he drew his sword.

The wind with its swooshes of coolness was gentle and the branches of the trees moved ever so slightly as it filtered its way in and out of the tangled bunches of limbs; they were dark dismal hemlock unlike any that I had ever seen before in my life; and it appeared to be a solemn day with a hint of darkness on the inside of the forest, but sunny and bright out in the clearing where we stood erect.

As I looked as deeply inside in the function of my focus and a bit of strain to the presence of my eyes; my brows and squinted retina caused pain on my forehead to the point of making me just a little dizzy.

I stood back and shook some of the unclear focus and wetness from my full and dark eyes, the strength of their tightness stretched them until a couple blood vessels broke sending sharp dagger like surges into my head and penetrate my brain so deeply that my thoughts were only to sit down upon one of the fallen ash trees to pull the stress from my head.

My powers were limited enough the way it was and since I needed more powers than I already had inside of me, I felt weak in not only body, but mind and spirit as well.

If I were to use any of my witch powers to cast any spell, I would have to work extremely hard with limited resources that would be very demanding, and then it would have to be done with the utmost urgency as possible. I did not want any more stress than I was already under on the inside of my mind's eye, and prayed to my Father Sky and Mother Earth to lift the burden of weakness so that I could perform like an authority and not a mere armature witch of sort like I already felt I was.

My contents of pressure began to filter themselves out of my head, but before I totally recovered from the pressure one of the tree branches seemed to come alive and it grabbed my body and began to claw at me like some sort of demon; and as I looked at it, I started pulling hard at it to break it free from around my frail and weak flesh. The pain was excruciating, a bit embarrassing, irritating, and intolerably to the point of almost causing me to pass out.

The tree had appeared to have a hideous head with sharp teeth; its body had wings and legs as well as arms with hands and sharp claws protruding from them like daggers.

All of the sudden it seemed to be trying to pick me up and fly off with me. Its extended wings flapped hard, but were not strong enough to lift even little old me from the ground let, alone anyone else.

I let out a scream that made William turn just in time to see the demon tree clawing at me like a wild cat in heat. He immediately drew his sword and began to hack away at the tree. His blows were felt by the tree and its branches let go of me as one piece fell to the ground like a twig falling from the main base of its moss covered and lifeless form.

The deformed structure re-took its physical shape of a tree, but with one less branch than it had before. William and I looked at each other and knew this trek of our quest would be the hardest one thus far.

The two gay warriors were busy hacking away at the forest with all their humanly strength that they could muster up. As they did; a black goop flowed from the trees lifeless shapes like thick molasses; it had no odor, and when touched by our hands it did not feel sticky like molasses, but more on the order of blood, but what kind of strange blood was this that was black. I stopped and thought for a moment and knew that it was black because after all this was the Black Forest.

This phenomenon seemed more of a nuisance than anything else, but nonetheless we could not make any headway inside the Black Forest with just swords. I needed to use my powers somehow, but how was the main issue?

All of this quest thus far had made me forget that William had the Book of Shadows stored inside his pack, but after a few moments, I realized that he had left his pack on his steda, and we had left it and the other stallions tied up next to water and foliage several days behind us; how stupid can any one person be I thought to myself.

Now how was I to tell my Dear William that he had left the book behind when we really needed him to bring it with us so I could use it on not only Stella and the Dragon, but in other matters like this one before us without a moments notice?

It seemed to me like he would have had the common sense enough to bring it, but sometimes men can be really dim-witted once in awhile like William, and others like Clancy and Hemsley; well need I say more.

"William, I believe that now would be a good time to bring forth the Book of Shadows so I can use it against this magical Black Forest, would you not think so my kind sir?" I knew he would try and default in the matter and claim that he has it in his haversack, but when he looked for it, he discovered that he indeed had left it behind.

Now we would be set back a week; and I commanded that and Sir Clancy and Sir Hemsley be the ones who would go back and fetch it while my Dear William and I stay here by the Black Forest until they returned to join back up with us.

"As you command Princess Yvonne, we are at your service and shall make it as quickly as humanly possible." Clancy spoke up as if he were the spokesperson for both he and Sir Hemsley and then he agreed by just bowing his head ever so slightly.

I knew that neither one was pleased to make the trek back and then do it all over again, but to me it did not matter, this would give William and I lots of time alone, and them too for that matter if they choose to, and somehow I knew that they too would be engaged in their yucky sexual behavior while William and I made our own sweet and real musical black magick right here in never-never land.

It would be a treacherous trek with many more unforeseen and hidden dangers and despite their gayety with a lighthearted and lively feeling for one another along with a bizarre way of behaving showing such physical and spirited activity as if it were some sort of joyful festivity of sort.

The red and yellow sun was at its peak in Father Sky as Mother Earth, myself and William settle back for some relaxation; looking onward as the two gay warriors prepare themselves for a round trip of fun and excitement in this new found promise land of the eastern sector of beasts, monsters, and just plain weird and strange creatures like merrow, smooze, and ogre jelly, and now these magical hemlock trees. I sat there thinking; what other sorts of creatures might be lurking near by and beyond this forest so dense that hinder our way forward to victory.

William and I had to take shelter from the elements, but where?

I looked all around me and all I saw was the past pieces of scenery as well as what lay in front of us; the odd Black Forest, but nothing beyond my nose outside of William and myself, because our two peculiar and uncanny companions were completely out of our sight.

I knew that if we stayed too close to the trees that they would come alive from the feel of warmth from our hot blooded bodies, and then grab us, squeezing us lifeless and devour our remains once liquefied, even the fallen ones that would normally be dead and on the verge of rotting into dust were still alive and well, and we would not be able to use any of their parts to make a shelter with.

Stones were our only hope to make a moderately complete wall and protect us somewhat; providing we could gather enough and stack them accordingly in a circular format and create an igloo of sort, but what would we use for the top section to finish it off?

William and I walked hand in hand for a short bout, and the task of gathering big stones was a little distasteful in my mind's eye, but never the less we had to work our asses off to get 'er done in time before nightfall came upon us.

Much to our bolt from the blue we came upon some fine bushes that would be useful to cover our igloo shelter once we completed its walls, and they would also make us a mighty fine bed to lay on after we took our pelts and furs off to throw over them for our completed bed.

"Look William, there is some excellent bushes and just what the sage needs to cure our stressful task at hand." I was subtle and as lady like in my mannerism as I could be and began to gather some big stones as my frail and lustrous-bosomed body would allow me to carry to a short hillside near by our current location in the never-never land of the east.

Picking up five or six; William joined in and brought the much larger ones and began to mound them on top of one another with such caution as not to make then topple back down and create a mess. He seemed to know how to construct an igloo shelter for some odd and unusual reason, but at my teenage years everything seemed odd and unusual, maybe because I was not quite mature enough to even make good enough decisions on my own yet, and I knew that I sure did have a long way to go in growing up to be a responsible adult.

I knew I was not any kind of construction worker, nor a laborer; because my strength was giving up on me after carrying about a couple dozen or so rocks and placing them next to our makeshift igloo asylum.

William showed me how to use his sword to cut branches from the bushes for our sanctuary away from all of the insanity of this crazy world we were in while he finished gathering the rocks and placing them in the fashion of our igloo. That made me much happier and not as trite as I was just a few moments ago. I began to place the turquoise branches on top of the portion that William had completed; and one by one the stone and bush igloo took on its own temperament.

Soon it was finished and much to my amazement it actually looked like something that would be useful in our future, and if it stood the elements of time we could use it on our return jaunt back to our motherland of Alexandria.

Night was upon us and a blue mist formed in our faces bringing along with it a sudden chill, but it was a warm night and I could not believe the strange weather patterns that formed in this part of Angleland.

William had took some branches and formed a door by tying them together with one another in a woven fashion just like our clothing was tied together, and it was an admirably brilliant design if I might say so myself; after all I did help create it.

My bones ached from the top of my head to the bottom of my feet, but we had it done and out of our hair before it took to total darkness with the shadows of the Black Forest dripping themselves down upon us

77

in wait for our approach when we were ready to finally move from our igloo asylum and enter into their domain; a domain of fatality to all who dare enter the thicket of blackness that hide inside it things that one would only dream of in nightmares.

Once inside our safety nest, we took off our top furs and placed them upon a bed of soft turquoise branches that shimmered from the glow of our vanilla incensed candles; creating a soothing atmosphere of safety, warmth and total relaxation.

We settled down for the night knowing that we were as safe as a new born baby in its mothers arms.

It was a quiet night in the cold mountainous region of the east where strange things happen unexpectedly without warning.

We lay on a slightly lumpy but cozy bed of turquoise branches and top furs from our attire and listen to the gentle breeze whisk by our igloo, and as it did, I could almost hear it whisper in my ear..."Whooooo areeeeee youuuuu upooooon myyyyyyy moooooouuntain tooooop thattttttttt dissssstuuuuuuuuuuuuuurbbbbb meeeeeeeee." It sent chills all over my body, and I held onto William with a warm assurance of being secure from all such matter that echo its words of dissatisfaction into my teenaged brain.

"William, I am happy that it was you who came into my life that day, for you are the only man who can satisfy my needs." I said; as I lay as close as I possibly could without crawling inside of him for more security I thought how nice it would be if we were in Castle Davenport in my cozy bed instead of here in a land of threat, misery, worry, and unforeseen jeopardy.

"I too am glad it is you who summoned me that day in our village and needed me on this your quest to save all of our people and your loyal subjects. It must have been my destiny, preordained for the future. Somehow I feel it was predetermined in my birth to be with you Yvonne who is a beautiful Princess, almost a woman, but on top of all of that you are a true lady in every since of the word." It was an inevitable series of events that happen to both of us with an inner realizable purpose of a life filled with ups and downs as well as many challenges in addition to the inner purpose of a life itself that was discovered and realized inside of our destiny to be with one another no matter what happened along the path to happiness, love and well being.

Some of the branches were poking me in not only my back, but also in places they had no business poking me in, and that made me a little uncomfortable knowing that both of us were so damned tired that making love now would only make us more miserable as well as uneasy with each other, and I just had to live with it unless I wanted to argue with my sweet and loving Dear William, and I sure was not about to do that.

We lay their silent trying to sleep, but sleep would not come because we were not only too tired, but restless and had lots of uneasy feelings flowing through our blood streams like ripples on a pond in late spring.

Things on the dragon front were progressing much better for Stella than she thought they would ever have progressed over the years, but her favorite dragon-Black, was proving to be an excellent student; but the only draw back was the use of his stud to the three huge bitches of his breed, and she would get furious from time to time because she wanted him to mate so that her lair would be full of new hatchlings that would turn into beautiful babies for training at an infancy stage.

Black was not living up to Stella's expectations, nor her standards when it came down to him making love to his potential bitch mates next door to him in the cave. She could not show him how to use his huge organ make it with the three bitch dragons, because she herself had never had a male mate with her.

The three bitches were in the sector next to his containment cage behind the limestone stalactite pillars hanging from the cave roof, not its sister the stalagmite on the cave floor that had been magically transformed into razor sharp malachite pillars of petrified steel bars that interlocked in a woven manner so to keep him and the female dragons at bay.

His cage stood alone, and separated by several layers of magical barbed stone structures of razor sharp malachite, but with the use his fire breathing ability he sometimes made a few of them to melt, but before he could complete his task of disintegrating them completely; Stella would rush in at the sound of Black's roar and the gastric odor from the razor sharp stalactite and stalagmite bars melting like the raw material they had been transformed from in her foundry of magical spells.

Now the three female bitches were showing some good signs and a little bit of promise in their training, but Black was her first captured dragon and he was the king of his kind when it came down to its destructive powers as well as him having great battle skills.

One of the female dragon was not a fighter unless confronted by the Black dragons closeness to her, then she would almost rip him to shreds with her claws and teeth; she was a real bitch, even more-so than the bitch witch Stella herself was; none the less she too had some degree of potential in a fight, but not in love making, or in mating with the Black Dragon and have off breed of herself.

Black and the other three dragon have many different body parts and features; they all have sturdy skeleton structures with well-built heads, extended neckline where Stella had placed a huge handcrafted sword point steel spiked collar and attached long chains like those that hold a ships anchor to them so they could not fly away very far even if they did escape before her training was completed; she knew they would have to return to their lair for shelter sooner or later.

They all had broad shoulders, solid legs, and tails so strong that they would break a person in half if they would hit someone with their scaly mass, and they were all equipped with very considerably sized wings.

As we lay there on the branch and fur bed inside our makeshift igloo shelter, William began to tell me about what a dragon was really like, and how we would die if captured by a dragon's massive head; burnt to a crisp, and eaten alive without mercy.

"If one of Stella's dragons were to catch a human being like us in its muscular jaw they would not swallow us whole, but would spike us first with their snake like fangs, fling us high into the air, and if it has the ability to throw flames at us we would be hot roasted meat ready to re-catch and then chew us up with their massive omnivore molars and slide our ground up flesh into its belly to be digested and then make us into manure and spew us back out onto the ground to rot away in time along with the rest of the crap in its world."

"Ohhhh, how horrible a death that would be." I almost heaved my jerky, wine and bread, but held my gagging throat so not to make a real mess all over us or our hide-a-way from danger as well as the sometimes in climate weather in these parts of my dear Angeland.

William continued to tell me about dragons, and I could not sleep from the intrigue of his dragon's tales; even though I knew a little about them from seeing one once as it flew over my beloved Alexandria.

"Now, as I said its wings are huge and very strongly built, and the wind from their flapping would be almost like that tornado that we just encountered, but a whole lot worse, mainly because of their colossal flight physique that has bruit force behind them to lift their mass high into the heavens with the power of their thin leathery skin that covers their bony wings. You can see right throw some of their wings if the light hits them just right, but when the light is away from them, it is impossible to see their structure." William took a brief pause to catch his breath from the altitude that we were at; giving me an opportunity to speak a few words so that he would continue his tales about these mystical creatures.

"How is it that you are so knowledgeable about dragons my prince?" I hesitated so I could force him to continue talking, because I was still a little bit frightened.

"Yvonne, I have had an opportunity to view one of these creatures up close years ago when I was about your age. It was a green dragon that had been cornered by some of my villagers back in my homeland of Welsh. My father and some other men had it trapped against a walled in canyon, in addition to the fierce battle they put up against the beast they could not kill it. The battle lasted several hours and most of my fathers men had been killed as well as devoured by the demon dragon, not to mention the massive quantities of the dragon's - flying poop that it had splattered all over the place that smothered dozens of really good people; men, women and children without any preference in it demeanor. I stood behind a boulder watching them being eaten alive one by one, and my father knocked unconscious, but before the dragon could fly away I saw how it was built, and the odd thing was it looked like it was heavy with infant." He took another deep breath of air as he popped his head out of the make-shift doorway letting some of the chill inside our igloo making me shiver ever so slightly.

"William I am cold, come here and warm my body and tell me more. I do not want any beast to see us." I shook like a leaf on an ash tree and millions of goose pumps spread themselves all over my body like a disease.

William closed the doorway and crawled back beside me and I snuggled next to his body for warmth once again and I could feel his warm blood as he covered himself back up to take the chill away from his own body along with mine.

Once we were snuggled up close enough I leaned my face toward his cheek and gave him a big kiss.

"Thank you William. Now tell me more about dragons, they are such an interesting subject matter." I lay silent next to my betroth taking deep breaths of cool crisp air and listened to his heart beat and his valuable words about dragons and knew once I had the Book of Shadows in my hands and the time was right; his knowledge that he had given to me would be most valuable to me.

"As I grouched behind that boulder looking at that big green beast I kind of felt sorry for it because it was all cut up from the many sword slashes, but the most revealing cut was across its outsized stomach. Blood flowed from the gash and the dragon let out a roar that shook even that boulder that I was hiding behind."

"Do go on my Dear Willy; I like you talking to me with your wisdom this way." I Moved my head back and forth across his hairy chest a few times and settled myself back into his hypnotic trance of words that gave be the strength that I needed to fight my battle of spells towards the dragon and my evil step-sister Stella the devilish witch of the eastern sector.

"As I said my love, I watched very carefully; my eyes were as big as buggy wheels and got even bigger as the dragon began to give birth. It was not like other animals of its kind who lay their eggs in a nest; no not this one; no maim, she gave birth like a cow or even a human female does through her sexual organs between its legs. It let our several more roars that were more like thunder than pain roars, and as it did I watched as the baby dragon slid out onto the ground all slimy and full of blood and began to inhale blue flames from its mouth. I could not tell what color it was at first, but as it wobbled itself up from the fetal position it was as coal black as night, and more like the coal in color that we use from the ground back in Alexandria." William crawled back to the door and opened it once again taking still another breath of fresh crispy fairy's –witch mountain air and then re-closed and began to slide himself back to where I was laying all warm and cozy under the furs.

"That sounds out of the ordinary to me. A Green Dragon giving vaginal birth to a Black Dragon. How is that possible?" I could hardly believe what my psyche was absorbing through their wax filled gills that were attached to the side of my cranium.

"Yes, it did seem unusual to me at that time as well, on the other hand now that I think of it, dragons do come in different species, and on top of it; I can remember that occasion like it was an earlier epoch of geology and a division of the period between the Holocene and Pleistocene epochs of the quaternary period and is characterized by rock formation that separated mammal from aquatic vertebrate with gills; those cold-blooded animal that typically has jaws, fins, scales, a slender body, a two-chambered heart, and gills for providing oxygen to the blood. In other words of a more common language so you will understand Yvonne, I mean simply fish, but they evolved into a much more land worthy creature with legs and so forth. Now that I think of it; our astronomical moments in time are arbitrarily chosen as a reference point for defining the position of celestial bodies causing change in many different types of amphibian and mammal alike to become infant baring land creatures such as dragons." William was a real talker once he got started on a subject that was of interest to him. I began to yawn and get a wee bit sleepy, but sheep would not come to my weary eyes for fear had already set its foot up my crawl hole and settled down for the long hall.

"How interestingly put my Dear William; yes how interesting indeed… awwwweeeuuuhum." I began to faint slowly into his lap and soon I was fast asleep to the unknown world of my brain in addition to the outside influences that bestow themselves at our doorway.

That night, as I lay there dead to everything except my sub-conscious the nightmarish thoughts overcome my reasoning and made me toss and churn like a whirl pool until I awoke the next morning all sweaty and so fearful that I hid my eyes beneath the cozy furs with the exception of peeping out several times to see if any danger lurked near by our igloo shelter.

The night went faster than I wanted it to go, but now that it was daylight, and I could see what was near by us I slowly slithered from beneath them and back out into the reality of my mind's eye.

The fireball was popping up over the ridge; shimmering hot and penetrating into my flesh, creating a great deal of needed heat to draw the nights chill from my bones.

I so much wanted to know more about these mystical creatures known as dragons, especially the green one.

William had told me shortly after the green dragon gave birth to its young one that it flew away, leaving the little Black dragon to fend for itself. I thought, how sad; how could a mother leave its young alone in such a cruel and ruthless environment as this. William did not say another word about it as the day progressed.

We built a small blaze so that we could heat some of our provisions. After that we kept a close watch on not only the Black Forest, but our entire surroundings so we would be able to detect any dangerous creature that might approach our encampment.

The next thing I knew, my dear sweet Willy went behind another boulder to relieve himself, but the smell was atrocious as it breezed by my nostrils on its way out toward the mighty forest. William was taking way too long, but the odor kept on drifting towards where I had my backside perched on a petrified tree shaft. I called to him several times with bearhtm (a twinkling of an eye) tone, but had no immediate response, and began to get worried a wee bit about him. I decided to shift my way a little closer, thinking that maybe he did not sit in judgment with his facial gills.

"Willy." I said with wonder in my vocal cords. "Are you alright love?" Slowly I began to peek behind the boulder and there was William pooping his backside off, it was runny, smelly, and downright gross in nature to look at, and I turned my head away as soon as he started to look up to see who was near by him.

"Is that aaahhhhhuuuuuhhhh you Yvonne?" His grunting was so loud that it caused him not to hear me calling him from a distance.

"Yes, it is I, Yvonne…your princess, love." I held my nose and my breath the best I could so that I would not inhale any more of his gastric fumes that lay within the liquefied green slime upon the ground beneath his rolled down leather and fur hide pants.

"Pe-yew, that is a very bad smell love. What was it that caused you to run in such an awful manner as you are?" I did not pretend that I had seen him, because my actions out-weighed my words.

"I do not know love, but my insides feel as though they are coming out my ass." His could not hold back the flow of runny mess and he continued to groan and grunt with much pain.

I started to head in reverse while facing his direction and told him that I would wait for him inside our igloo hut, that the smell was way too atrocious for me to handle any longer.

He began to clean himself off with as many leaves from a near by bush as he could in order to clean off his butt.

William showed up several minutes later holding his belly like he had nothing left on its insides and he kept scratching his ass from time to time. Little did either of us know that the leaves he wiped with were poison ivy leaves? Spoon he broke out in a rash that spread all over his body and all I could do was cover him up with as many furs as I could and keep the chill off of him. I had no cure but did manage to find some water near by. So I took one of our pelt sacks that had some of our wine in it at one time and filled it with as much water as I possibly could so that I could cleanse him and give him the necessary nourishment he needed to sustain life and make most of the rash dissipate with time.

As I attend to him, my thoughts run wild like a pack of wolves on the prowl. I could not believe all the bad things that has happened to us on this quest in such a short time. I know he will be alright in time, but for now I have to try and use my spell powers to cure him of this rash, before our companions get back with the Book of Shadows in two days time; I pray they do anyway.

Sir Clancy and Sir Hemsley were back to where they tied the steda, and were about to disembark for the trek back to join up with Hemsley and I on top of the mountain but before they had a chance to get up the first leg of the jagged mountainside, a couple Ogre Barbarian were prowling the terrain to see who had killed part of their clan on top of the mountain. They seemed madder than a rabid tornado as they pounded the ground with their tremendous weight and size that was in combination with their strength that makes Ogres almighty barbarians of the natural kind. It was one of the leaders of the Ogre population that had dwindled at our hands who took on the task to search the countryside with his brother Ogre from a neighboring clan of lesser barbarians. These two monstrous bruits had spotted Hemsley and Clancy and began to pound their way across the ground at lightening speed and were soon upon them with a fury, and at the always ready position for a battle that would be truly formidable.

"Look out Clancy we have some guests." Hemsley shouted as he looked down where Clancy had placed himself in a small ridged crevice with one hand above his head ready to take hold of the next safest handhold. But it was too late.

The Ogre leader had leaped high into the air and took hold of Clancy's foot and gave it a big heave that forced him to let loose of the sharp malachite spear, and as he did; it ripped his hand to shreds and had completely severed three of his fingers. Blood gushed out with a flow like fresh volcanic lava. He let out a scream that sent chills all over my spinal cord and was buried deep into my brain. Clancy knew he had no real chance to survive once a Barbarian Ogre had you totally in its clutches, so he quickly pulled the book from beneath his cloak and gave it a hardy heave ho to me on the next ledge about four feet or so above where he had been perched before he fell brutally back down to the ground a bloody mess.

I grabbed the Book of Shadows and scurried to the next highest level where I knew that the other monstrous Ogre could not reach me if he were to make an attempt to bounce toward me. I looked down at Clancy who was making every effort to fight the big ugly Barbarian Ogre; he yelled so loud that it made as echo throughout the mountains and rebounded back to penetrate my ears like a banshee was inside my ears, the beast had already pulled his arm completely off and had tossed it aside like an unwanted bone from a deer or some other unfortunate animal that had been slain for meat.

Clancy yelled at the top of his lungs once again, but it did not do him any good because there was nothing more he could do except that. He had already lost control of his sword that was in the hand of the other beast who just looked at me growling as he picked up Clancy's severed arm and began to gnaw on it like an uncooked soup bone.

The lead Ogre took a bite out of his face and spat it on the ground beside him and tried to take a hand hold on the ledge but cut its hand all to pieces from the malachite ridges and began to yell up ad me with his thunderous voice.

"Me get you soon human, you see, you wait see, me get you like me get this one." He headed toward his companion and began to share Clancy with him like the wild wolves and other predatory animals do after a fresh kill.

I heard the leader say as I climbed even higher and out of their sight, and watch our steda scurry away so they too would not be devoured by the Barbarian Ogre like Clancy had just been.

"This human good food, me want more, me want the one that escape, but me get he soon." They gnawed hardily on Hemsley's friend and short time lover making a mess all over their faces as Hemsley climbed higher and higher as fast as the sharp mountain spears would allow him to do and soon he was at the cave level where he could rest for a short while, because he knew that he did not have much time to get back to his traveling companions and tell them what had happened to his best friend as well as to give the book to Yvonne so she would be able to use it against her controlling evil step sister Stella and the demon Black Dragon of the east.

Hemsley was exhausted to no end and knew he needed rest before he could even attempt the long climb up the next level to meet up with Yvonne and William so they could get on with their quest to end this Hell they were all in and start life fresh once more, that is if they all survived this territory of monsters and the likes. He decided to take a chance and seek safety in a near-by cave and hopefully it would not contain any bizarre, strange, uncanny, or peculiar oddities.

Night was almost upon them once more and Hemsley huddled up next to the cave opening as close as safety would let him be and fell asleep with tears in his eyes from the loss of his friend and lover.

As I sat next to William, I thought and thought of a cure spell for my lover, but I too drifted off into the never land of nightmares and wondering dreams from thinking so hard about a cure spell for William's poison ivy rash on mainly his ass, as well as the rest of his hard body.

The Take Away Poison Spell

"I summon the powers of the weed that has poison in it to be cast out of its branches

Morning of the dirt that grows flowers that heal, cast it out of this persons flesh

Make no haste, make no spare time, do it now

I have my Mojave Desert dust effective; and I make it useful to the branches of rash and sting

Power of dark undo this disease that had made my man so miserable with itch, I am the good witch of day and want it soothed here before the clay.

Mojave Desert dust be blown into the patches that have a hold on flesh and undo your evil now. Magick leaf of berry bush give a hand of time and do it now.

I command you to end this moment of rash on flesh that you have a hold of now, I cast you out and make his flesh pure once more and enter there-in so that he will be cured for eternity and may I take possession of you that has held him captive; I command you to leave and make him whole and strong once more in a twinkling of an eye from the calico cat and blind the black cat of poison ivy to make it a berry bush instead."

The rash left as soon as I placed my hand on William's ass, and he sighed like a new born baby with relief from the pains of growth and stretched flesh that once bore a terrible rash where a person has to defecate from in the time of need.

As daylight broke in my eyes, I began to get drowsy and was about to fall asleep when William awoke and placed his arm around my waist for comfort in his spirit. It placed comfort in my spirit as well when I looked at his ass and other body parts before I crawled beneath the fur pelts beside him, the rash was completely gone from his entire body and it was pure once more, but the funny thing was, William now smelled like berries from a raspberry bush in the summer sun.

I could not help myself but to laugh out loud just a tiny smidgen; William looked at me and only smiled and then fell back to sleep holding me as if tomorrow may never come. I could not help but place that same smile upon my visage.

The sun was creeping slowly upward into the clouds that were burning away with each spark from the suns mighty rays, and the heat was making itself known to our souls once more as I drifted off into a slumber land of fantasy and pleasant dreams.

I awoke from my deep trance to discover William sitting outside of our igloo shelter, no shirt, no shoes and making service to a fire that held a freshly caught northern goose from a flock that was flying overhead honking their fool heads off as to say. "Hey, I see you far below, but we are out of your arrow range and you will never get any of us for your bellies." But it was too late; William had already brought one down to Mother Earth and was roasting it on a brilliantly lit fire for our noon meal.

The others had already flew off with much commotion in their squawking honks as they flapped their plume wings to the sound of each others beat; speeding off to the northern sector of our great show covered lands to do what ever it is that geese do after many days journey of flight before making a smooth landing on the many ice and snow filled ponds for a well deserved rest.

One was more than plenty of food for our bellies and we would have enough left over for our night time meal as well.

The day was hot and long, and we had nothing to do except eat and hide ourselves inside our igloo away from the penetrating rays of the sun that was already high in the sky in all of its glory immaculately downward on our domain to help bring forward new life beneath as well as above the grounds we trod upon in our daily lives.

Sir Hemsley was slowly making his way back to our campsite; tired sore and full of marks from the Ogre's mighty battle blows as well as from him trying to escape certain death so to provide food for the cannibalistic and barbarian monsters of the mighty mountain that I shall now dub Mount Birmingham of London.

Hemsley had made his way to the edge of the last plateau that filtered itself into the slopes of the mountain that we were encamped upon for the past several days and as he edged his limp and torn up body over the last set of spiked malachite stalagmites he collapsed in the heat of the mighty suns rays. The temperature must have already reached well over one hundred Celsius and was climbing even hotter as the day progressed.

He had shed most of his wool pelts and was down to the baer essentials as he lay in the sands of the rolling dunes atop of Mount Birmingham of

London; his flesh was blistering with hundreds of water boils and as red as freshly cut beets ready for further cooking for a hot snack for bar barbarian Ogre and his company, but since he was so high up the mountain, the cannibals could not make snack out of his hot blistered flesh.

Evening soon came and the sun was sinking behind the top of our mountain and Hemsley awoke in immense pain. His tortured body pulled in all directions as he walked slowly towards the campsite where Sir William and I was laying in wait for him to bring me the Book of Shadows to study so I can fix all of our problems within a matter of hours once the opportunity prevailed before me and my comrades in arms.

As he approached I could feel my witch powers returning into my mind and my body began to gain strength as well. I started to feel like my old self once more and no longer a little child at play with some newly developed powers to test the waters with.

As nightfall bounced in our faces so did Sir Hemsley. His tormented and tortured flesh had shown their scars in my eyes as he came close to the campfires light. He looked just horrible, like a waling dead man straight out of the grave; he took one last step and then fell to the ground beneath my feet. I immediately knelt down beside him along with William and began to tend to his battle wounds, water blister boils and reddened flesh.

He moaned and groaned, and screamed like a pig being slaughtered for market as he lay upon our bed of branches and fur pelts inside our igloo shelter.

We worked on him throughout the night as well as keeping watch over the terrain so no beast or slithering amenorrhea creature would bother us while we took turns sleeping to the extent of what was humanly possible under the extreme circumstances before our weary souls.

That night brought much unearthly clatter that echoed through-out the Black Forest and crept their way deep inside my mind's eye; moans of death seemed to scream amongst the vine laden with black mucus like slime dripping down a mad wolf's face after a fresh kill; it was crammed with blood curling scratches that covered an entire slate rock while sinister claws dug their way into some ones flesh ripping out cuts in order to devour the prime ribs that lay beside them and then slash into the very heart and soul of their poor victims to snatch vital organs like livers, spleen, gizzard, lungs and last the throbbing, agonizing and tender heart.

Another night passed by me allowing little sleep to sooth my weary judgment to almost the peak of exhaustion and I knew that I must remain strong in heart, mind and soul so that I would be able to study the Book of Shadows enough to destroy both the demon Black Dragon and my evil step-sister Stella the wicked witch of the east.

My eye lids drooped and sagged like bread doe being molded into a shape like that of a wilting hierarchy, but I done what I must to pull my band back together once again and save my face despite my ills of weariness from the lack of much needed sleep.

Chapter 7
Through the Forest of Magick

The next morning also came way too quickly for me; I was so exhausted; my eyes so heavy with wanting sleep, and my soul wanted to flee this nightmarish hell that we had traveled to on the quest to cure my people of the Black Plague; that Black Death that had befallen upon my village; and from all the evil spells that my wicked - satanic step-sister of mine; Stella had betokened upon us in this baron and forsaken land high on Mount Birmingstone London that lay three or four days journey from Alexandria Angleland.

Sunrise was earlier than normal, and I knew that that bitch witch Stella was already at work planning her next phase to slow us down, or kill us one, and I had to get a little sleep and much needed rest in order to not only read the Book of Shadows, but to use its spells to their fullest against that sleaze-bag of a step-sister of mine; Witch Stella and her pet peeve the Black Dragon.

"William, it looks as though Sir Hemsley is getting better, so we must build me a small shelter so I can get some sleep, or I will not be of any good to any of us when the time comes for us to fight our evil foes my step-sister and her demon dragon in a couple days from now; I must rest for another day. We have came a long way and have under-went many horrendous obstacles to make it this far, and I for one am not going to turn back, not now nor ever until our quest has been completed. One more day will not matter all that much my love; so let us get busy on my lean-to against the wall of that cliff over there okay." I was firm in tone, but used my feminine charm to make sure it was done immediately before the suns rays beat us to death once again.

Sir Hemsley lay steadfast asleep in our igloo where his wounds could heal so he would be semi strong enough to continue with us on the rest of my quest to the dragon's lair the next day.

I knew that while I was in the lean-to I could also study the Book of Shadows enough to cast their spells against my bitch step-sister and that feces faced dragon of hers. That was mostly all that was on my mind, and I would not be completely at rest till the deed was done and they were both dead and out of my hair for all eternity.

It did not take very long to construct the lean-to, but we had to exercise every bit of caution so that we would not gather any of the slithering branches from the magical Black Forest because I was not about to let myself die before my time and mission was completed that was one thing for certain.

"Yvonne, this is a perfect place for you to lay your precious body down for your much needed rest and sleep. I will keep lookout as well as tend to Sir William in our igloo so that he will not disturb you." William had every intention to make me a shelter before I had mentioned it to him, but said nothing to me because he knew that since I was exhausted that I might jump down his throat for trying to take charge of the situation at hand, and more-so he knew that I was his princess, lover and ruler, and anything I said was law and he must obey my every command.

Within an hour he had a fine lean-to and a worthy shelter built for me; I could hardly wait to snuggle up inside to rest and read a good book, the ultimate book in all of this my realm; the Book of Shadows.

I was intrigued with all the sinister spells; some were suggesting pure evil while others threatening or suggesting malevolence, menace, and ultimate harm to the receiving person of such wonderful spells as these that lay before my mind's eye. I could use all of them when and where I so choose; and no one could stop me.

Finally I had all of my powers back; and now I had every witches dream right in my clutches; the Book of Shadows. No other witch could even dare challenge me now except that bitch step-sister of mine Stella, and as my mind grew stronger I now knew that I would be even more powerful than Stella ever could be

Her and her puny pet peeve of a black dragon would be no match for me now, and that made me as happy as a tic on a boar, or a leech on some poor retched beggar in the streets of Alexandria could ever be.

I searched the entire book for a spell that would see us through the spellbound Black Forest that hindered our way to where my foe was hiding. I just did not care how tired I was now, and read more than I had ever done in my entire sixteen years of life here upon my Mother Earth, and it felt good to my soul.

Soon I came upon a pathway spell that would clear the way for me and my companions to safely pass the enchanted black trees of demons.

Safe Passage through the Unknown Spell

"Wonderer of the unknown, I challenge you with sword more powerful than held captive in stone.

Cut a path long and straight through the thick of trees before my feet so I and those with me shall pass in safety this day and for eternity.

Let no foe, nor evil bright spark, nor beast of any sort follow this my path beyond and safely back to this the beginning of my slashed pathway.

Take my horde by your hands; lead the way; destroy any evil inside the trees and cast them to drop in dry rot onto the ground; so to never harm others any more throughout eternity and beyond.

Safe passage through the unknown I cast thy cutting edge of your sword now."

As soon as I made the cast, I watched the trees split apart making a magic path through their evil thicket and I listened to their screams as they wilted into dust upon the pathway, and within a matter of minutes it was finished. I got up from my lean-to that had been made strong with a slanted roof that rested against the wall of a bloodstone cliff, and even though it was small, it fit me to a tee; as I watched in amazement from throwing a fine spell from my own powers, I felt prouder than I had ever felt in all of my life.

I knew for sure that I would soon defeat my enemy, my evil step-sister Stella and that meanest bitch in all our land along with the powerful black dragon.

Morning came fast, and my eye lids were drooping all the way to my knees, but I felt just fine, and was almost as strong as a bull ox or so it seemed to my mind's eye.

"Come on you two, let's get a move on now, you hear me, move your lazy asses." I was throwing my weight as hard as I possibly could as well as yelling at William and Hemsley, I kicked them both real hard in their butts and they both jumped almost a mile high from being stead-fast and sound asleep.

"Hey! Who the bloody blazes kicked my ass?" Sir William yelled as he flew out towards me with his sword drawn ready for battle.

"Save your strength for fighting the dragon alright." I yelled at him with a nasty tone.

Sir Hemsley gives the impression of being just fine now since he had plenty of rest as well as the necessary medical treatment from William.

"Who, who the hell kicked my ass?" He yelled at me with his sword drawn as well.

"I did, your Princess Yvonne, what are you two going to do about it." I made them both feel vulnerable to my strong command, and all they both could do was bow before me in humility.

"I am sorry Princess, I thought an Ogre was after me again, please I beg your forgiveness my Princess." Hemsley humbled himself before me.

William joined Hemsley in the same fashion, and then I commanded them both to rise and behold the pathway through the Black Forest. They were dumbfounded and flabbergasted at the same time, not knowing I had all of my witch powers and then some back inside of me the way it should be.

"I, Yvonne am now the most powerful of all in our land and through-out the entire world now, let no one challenge me, let no one harm me nor those I cherish." I was starting to show my true colors now, and it made my peacock feathers burst with pure ecstasy.

"My Princess; Yvonne, you are whole once more, and I am exceedingly ecstatic and will do your proposition with submission at your will my love." William was now being bolder and showed his colors in the face of sir Hemsley.

"Sir William, you are in love with the Princess now are you?" Hemsley smiled as he asked William before me his intention, and although his lover was gone at the hands of a mean old Ogre, Hemsley seemed to be subtle in his demeanor towards accepting life as it was at present.

"Yes, We love one another, and will be wed as soon as we retreat back to Alexandria once our quest is completed, and no one will interfere, nor stop us from our union, it is written in the stars and in our hearts that we be man and wife, and that I Sir William shall be Prince and so help Princess Yvonne rule not only Alexandria, Angeland, but the rest of the world as well if I have any say so in it." He boasted like a bull moose in heat, as he stood erect before Sir Hemsley and I, William was also as proud as a peacock spreading his plumage to the world.

Within the hour we were strolling through the path, but on both sides there were many evil moans and groans of death, and I knew that the Black Forest would soon be set free of the evil that held it captive.

I had no worry about our safety now and by the mid day sun we would be on the other side of the darkened forest.

Many objects had hindered my way, and now that I had powers beyond my normal supremacy; there would be no spell or foe that I could not conquer, and soon we would be right in my evil step-sister Stella's face, ready to seize her area by my mighty force; to take control of the dwelling lair of the Black Dragon and her fortress.

The force of our arms was now strengthened from my powers, and Stella's defeat would soon be my victory.

I knew we would have a mighty battle, but I had already cast a spell over all of us so that no harm would come to me or my two remaining comrades. I was master, and the control over all evil was mine totally, although much difficulty was yet to influence the many ultimate decisions that I would eventually have to face.

I had already been scorned once when I was laying naked under the stars near my humble but quaint dwelling near the equinox of my wonderful Castle Davenport when I was sold out, yes I was a sold out goddess-worshipping witch.

That bitch of a step-sister had influenced my mother and father about a year before their death and told them I taught her how to be evil, and introduced her to spells that she could use to enhance her Craftiest powers so that she could be the ultimate Princess and not me.

Stella, had already trod on me once to the tune of pure evil in her Craftiest practices and brought many wicked spells to our household shortly before our parents passed to the great beyond of spirits, but thank the mighty creator of myself and all of my people that she got caught by our mother and set out of the castle for eternity; leaving the way for me to become Princess and ruler of all those and the land I dwell in.

I vowed to myself that I would not be bewitched, nor sold out ever again, and that I would not be a woman who was conquered, and controlled by someone or something that is difficult to overcome for their own gain and public expenditure.

It was difficult enough for me being a teenaged sixteen year old girl headed towards womanhood let alone being a powerful witch; and now the most ultimate and high princess of all times. I had the admiration and the love from the most handsome man in all of my land.

My affection, love, and strength of character along with my seductive powers of the heart had conquered William's complete spirit; and Stella would never in her wildest imagination ever steal him away from me, and as far as that demon dragon; it would never take my life away from me either. I truly had it all now, and soon I would be victorious and finally be able to set my people free of the Black Plague or Black Death as we call it in these parts.

I knew that once I destroyed Stella, and my two brave and noble knights slew the Demon Black Dragon and I cut out its dark heart and roasted the dead dragon's heart over brimstone from the volcano on the other side of my beloved Alexandria and I drank a small portion of its blood in a copper cup lined with pure gold, that I would have its mighty powers within me along with all of the witchery powers any Mother Goddess of witches would ever have inside of her; I knew that I would even be more powerful than my beloved mother; the Mother of all Goddess' Shauna whom has long since passed to the Great Father Sky to be with all of the ones of my father the great High Prince Zelstar of the Goddess' Gideon and all of my family who was also departed to that special realm amongst creator the Almighty God of all things living or not; and after eating the roasted heart of the dragon, I would be mightier than my father who was one of the bravest of all the knight's in our kingdom here in this my mighty Angeland.

The moans of the Black Forest seem to never let go and die out like they should with the howling of their fierce winds pierced our ears as though millions of people were being slain without just cause or reward of any sort; my head filled to its brim with those screams, those awful screams of the dead; I had to be strong enough so not to let my emotions show outward to my two travel companions; lest they think me mad like one of our village fools who rant and rave their insane non-sense to all who pass by them in order to gain their pity and give them shillings to hush their sometimes foul mouths.

About an hour later we were on the other side of the Black Forest and I thanked my Father Sky and Mother Earth for their mercy as well as my creator the almighty spirit whom I have heard so much about from foreign travelers who passed through Alexandria to distant shores and lands beyond mine.

"Yea, we art finally out of this horrid place of moans and the groans of the dead." I bolted out my words and paid no never mind to the strange looks that Sir Hemsley and my dear Sir William were giving me, but knew in my minds eye that they think me loosing my senses.

"Princess art ye alright." Sir William softly whispered as we made exit from the forest at last.

"Yea, that I am my brave friend; I just need rest for a short time that is all." My words were firm and stood true to meaning in response to my love Sir William.

"Yvonne, my love, are you sure you are alright; you look a bit peaked with your flesh showing a bit of weakness." William asked with a soft firm and mild mannered tone of voice.

"I… I that I am my dear William, I never felt better in my life thank God." I finally acknowledged that there was a God from my mind's eye to my travel companions.

"What is this strange word you have said my Princess; God; I have not heard such an oddity of language before. Is this new word something that you have made up?" Sir William was not too bright, and maybe he just had not heard strangers, or some of the other villagers speak it before, but I had to over look his ignorance at times just so I could keep him true to me and be my lover.

I sat down slowly on a rock and gazed at both William and Hemsley, and began to tell them all that I knew about this new spirit called God and his son Jesus that I someday would know personally and make our new religion in Angeland one of the Christian faiths that I have heard tell of.

"I have not made it up Sir William, it is said to be a true word, and according to those who pass through this our land tell how this God is our creator; and his son… this man that they called Jesus had died a horrible death on a thing they call a cross that he was nailed at both hands and his feet to it; they also told me that he was gouged in his side with a soldiers spear and had a ring of thorns placed upon his head its." I began to shed a couple tears as I began my tale, but slowly whipped them away before William and Hemsley seen them, and I yawned.

"This is mighty interesting my Yvonne, you must tell us more." William said with a bewildered gaze from his weary blue eyes.

"Yea, my Princess, it is an interesting subject indeed, I too want to hear more about this God who is supposed to be our creator, and his son this man called Jesus, but first we must finish this our quest." His focus was on slaying the demon Black Dragon and my evil step-sister Stella more-so than hearing about God and Jesus at this time, but at least I had them both curious enough to want to know more.

"I'm a free spirit here at last and I am now filled with various amounts of eclectic energy since we have departed this awful Black Forest. I must now tell you both some of the possessions I so much take pleasure in, but do not share…while I hide inside a wall of fantasy, it is just a masquerade for those who dare read my words. I am not a person who covers their self up with a dark side, and I am only who I am and not someone who takes things without due consideration. In some ways I am like this Book of Shadows; sometimes I am closed to all comers, yes even you my dear William, and sometimes I am open, and all it takes is someone to read the language of my face and body to see what it is that I am made of on the inside through your own mind's eye. I will enlighten you more now my dear William and you as well Sir Hemsley the gay and brave. Here are some of the things which I cherish on my insides, but do not take advantage of all that I say to you; least ye shall suffer the dire consequences of my wrath."

As we sat there, my thoughts drifted to other times and thoughts outside of what I really wanted to say to my dear friends about my plans that I had concerning converting our evil witching ways towards God and his son Jesus; this would come at a later time and place in our journeys.

"We had best stop for another day Yvonne my love; you look tired and need more rest so you can do your part of the battle with Stella and the Black Dragon!" William looked a little bit worried about me as he sat there with his puppy dog eyes flapping with the gentle breeze.

"You are right my dear William; Sir Hemsley and you must make us a shelter in that clearing over there and we will leave when day breaks tomorrow." I had chills in my voice from being so tired and did not want to argue, or display my childish manner to them, because after all I am a Princess as well as a young lady am I not?

I giggled just a slight bit as they began to pile up rocks and dead branches from some of the friendly trees outside of the Black Forest.

An hour later they had built two fine structures, one for William and me, and one for the still weary Sir Hemsley the gay brave warrior.

I sat lady like on a large log next to a fire that William started shortly before they made our shelters; my torn dress showed part of my sexy tight ass and one of my breasts showed a little as well, but I did not mind, it just enticed my dear William to want me more, and as far as Sir Hemsley, I knew he was not interested in the female physique, nor me, he would find himself another man once we returned to Alexandria in another week or so.

Once both men had sat themselves down before my feet, I began to ramble about myself and things that were dear to my heart, as well as things that I liked and so forth.

"My father's family hailed from this land, and my mother's and her family hailed from Egypt in on the continent of Africa. Both were around thirty-five and forty years old when they were taken away, but several years between their births. When it happened, but I remember their deaths well, especially that of my dear mother Shauna, but my father Zelstar was killed in a fierce battle with the Celtic people of Ireland. We have a long blood line that extends too many foreign shores, but none more precious to me than the line here in Angeland. I am very good at being relaxed in a conversation with a good friend, and so enjoy family gatherings, or at least I once did, but now I have no family here in this my land that I am aware of. I value many things, especially laughter, and sometimes even a private cry to help heal my inward spirit; ah… It does so bring a warm glow from the healing lights of my mind's eye, and radiates from the beyond where my dear parents dwell."

"I, Princess, 'tis pleasing to hear such feelings once again my Royal Highness." Hemsley moaned with a slight sigh and then smiled as he glared at the flames of the fire that began to brighten the darkness as it drawn near our place of peace and rest.

"I too Yvonne my love, 'tis heart felt, truly it is." William also sighed simultaneously with Hemsley, and also peered into the flames as I continued my thoughts.

"Honesty, and trust filled with morals of loyalty, being strict in my powers, and at the same time possess humor, but most of my virtues lay with my pleasures of erotic play and making love with the man I shalt love for eternity, and I will have no other, but be monogamous and faithful to him only; and I pray that he will be the same toward me."

William looked up from the fire at me and I at him, his sexy bedroom eyes seemed to say it all as did his smile, and he said with a soft tone.

"That I will my one and only true love… that I will promise you totally this day." He kept staring into my eyes, and I continued my thoughts once again, but did not mind interruptions from either one of my travel companions, because it made it all the more pleasurable to my thoughts.

"In the reality of my life there are a few things in which I indulge on a daily bases and they make me all the more proud of my mystical actions and my witches powers. I always try to be who I am – not what someone else wants me to be! I always try to make many memories that will last more than a lifetime, and I love so much sharing those memories with friends, but would enjoy this all the more if I had some of my extended family to share them with here, as I said before in this our beloved Angeland."

"Princess, may I ask to be released from your kind company for a brief moment, nature calls to my loins." Hemsley was not a bit shy in his words, and said what was on his mind no matter what was taking place at the time.

"You may Sir William." I said with a royal reply.

"Yvonne, I would also like to be relieved as well if you do not mind being alone for a very short time? It will not take long, that I also promise you my love, but you know how it is when the calling comes on ones vital organs!" He smiles with a sorrowful expression on his face, but I knew that it could not be helped.

"Yea, you may also be excused my love, but please hurry back, as there is still danger lurking out there in places we least expect them to be lurking." I showed more royalty in my words, and knew I was growing strongly into what I was destined to be, and that was a full pledged Princess and a real woman with much inward strength.

It was not long before both of them slithered their way back to the camp fire and before my eyes mostly for my protection per say.

Both men bowed before me as they approached, I expected it from Sir Hemsley, but not from my love William, but then again he too was still a warrior in my service, and that showed me that he too respected my authority as well as being my true love, and I would hold him to this mannerism even after we were married, that was one more thing I was sure of.

"You both may be seated in my presence." I smiled a real shit eating grin that made me gain more inward strength, even if I was only sixteen years of age, I was still in command and the Princess of all who were in my presence, even my love and soon to be husband; Sir William of Welsh.

Once more I continued my thoughts, and knew they would listen to everything I said before I would excuse them for the night.

"Life is only a mind game for all to play, and we are only the actors in life's little rolls on a daily basis. As I recall happy thoughts from my past, I also grow to appreciate the simple things life has to offer, even though I am filthy rich and wear rags at this moment. My best clothing is in my castle Davenport, and when we get back from this quest, I shall adorn my best royal gown and other luxurious garments for you both to feast your eyes upon, and then you will see true beauty like no other your eyes have ever feasted upon before."

Darkness drew closer and the moon had went to sleep behind some gloomy ominous clouds, and somehow I felt that something bad might happen real soon, but could not place my fingers on my entire feelings.

Appreciation of my friends meant lots to me; I continued my life story with a total open heart, and my past grew larger, and still larger right before my mind's eye; I was more happy since I had powers beyond my beliefs.

"I be fond of travel and much discovery of all new things that cross before me. Sometimes doing old things anew and sharing the experiences with good people like you my dear William, and also you my friend Sir Hemsley the brave gay fellow, and doing things that were once old and made new again only enables me to accept what simple pleasures that life has to offer me. Not all people have the ability to understand something the way that I am able to do, and that is to make positive change if not on someone other than myself, but change on myself at my own will and in due process. One must understand this be able to enjoy such wealth and reap there rewards." I was soft in pitch, and my attitude was pleasant and not under any stress so to say.

"I do not understand what it is you are talking about my princess, but your words do give me such pleasure and relaxation deep inside my mind, please do continue to fill my mind with your wisdom Princess Yvonne." Sir Hemsley was curious and not too well learned and I guess that I was; well a teacher and mentor to his child like understanding.

"Sir Hemsley, please do not interrupt whilst Princess Yvonne is speaking, it is sort of rude you know sir brave warrior." William was subtle, and you might say filled with intelligent, experience, and sensitivity enough to make such refined judgments and distinctions; he was ingenious in a small way, and cleverly roundabout with his words, but made his points very clear.

"I am pleased to know that you are sincerely interested in my wisdom Sir Hemsley, and I shall make you all the more wise if you do not interrupt me again is that clear." I had to be stern with him because after all he was child-like in his mind... hehehehehe.

"You know my dear William, I am well pleased at how you handle some things, and just being with you makes me at ease, and when we are alone together... doing what ever our fancies are to make us both happy, it tickles me so, and when your bravery protects me from the ugly things in life, these things make you my life partner, and the bitter seems all the more sweet than the latter." I gave him a slight wink from my eye, and a smile, along with blowing him a small kiss that I knew he so gratefully received.

"Thank you Yvonne and I feel the same when I am with you my love." William sure did know how to make a girl swoon, and his words almost made me faint with happiness, excitement, adoration, and infatuation; He knew deep inside that we were meant to be life partners and one unit for eternity.

Living life to the full extent to the bitter end as time passes us by, and to re-live it over and over again with my chosen mate who I shall gain much pleasure in for life through my eyes as I shall through his. We will endure any obstacle that confronts us, any foe, tragedy, or infliction of disease that tries to do away with our lives, and we shall prevail no matter what.

I do not mind being in the elements of rain, wind, snow and bitter cold with the one I love, just as long as we can see the beauty of it providing these are not of the extreme kinds of weather that Mother nature and Father time so often bring before us with such force and fury.

I have no regrets outside of that of loosing my parents, and not having close family near by me; I carry myself in my child-like manner, but yet being as a mature adult; I know what is good enough to take pleasure in, and what is not... life is a game many times over, and I will play it to win and not loose, because winning is to be in due course and to allow space, time for, and give rein to all of its tranquility and wrath.

I have tasted life, and have fallen from its path, but gained it back now that I have powers beyond belief, and it made me who I am this day; that makes me ecstatically filled with much happiness

"Let the storms in life come so that I may be able to kick it in its ass; let the hour class of life not run out of its sands so that I may be able to defeat my evil foes, and this beast of burden... the Black Death that Stella had brought to my people." My thoughts were firm and mi voice soft enough to the feelings of the spirit.

Life seems way too good to miss out on alone, I need total companionship until I reach my full potential, and meet my goal of destroying Stella and the Black Dragon, and I prayed to my mother and fathers spirit that no harm would come to my companions as long as we were on this quest. These two brave men were my heroes at the moment them I touch with out even touching flesh and they touch me in so many ways in the same way, with exception of my Dear William, who is allowed to touch me even in the flesh, but not Sir Hemsley, nor any other man as long as I am alive.

Growing up in sorrow and not having that special man in my life until Sir William came along made my life seem so useless, but now Ich am full enough, and yet have more to gain as time goes on; for I want a child to carry on my powers and name long after Ich am gone from this my Mother Earth.

"I like doing only what I like to do, and wonder if anyone else is doing the same things as I am doing or damned close to what I am doing. I so often wonder if we live in a parallel world, but wait, everyone else is doing the same as I... hanging on the web of life. I must be getting tired and will soon need rest as by tomorrow we shall reach the lair of my evil step-sister Stella and her mean spirited pet and demon Black Dragon... aahhhhhhhhhhuuuummm." I was getting sleepy, and nodded off a couple times without really realizing it, but kept talking so I could get everything out of my system.

I yawned once more… "AAaaahhhhhhhh Ummmmmm." and I lay down on some soothing furs so I could relax.

"Princess, may I speak? She nodded her head yes. "I beg… you had best get some sleeps we still have a half day journey to go before we reach our destination." Hemsley was such a gay gentleman, but always said exactly what was on his mind. He smiled gleefully.

"I will be alright Sir Hemsley, and I shall sleep when I am ready." I tried to be gentle on him, because he was one of my main fighting forces. I too smiled with cheer.

The night went slowly by and I was not in the least tired, or so I thought in my mind. Music danced in my head, and I began to sway with its melody, and hummed one of my favorite melodies, a lullaby that my dear mother hummed to me as a wee child.

"That is a pretty melody Yvonne… Do you know the name of it?" William gave me a soft smile with both his mouth and his gorgeous eyes and it soothed my soul all the more.

"It is called: Sleep Till Morning My Child, Sleep. Do you like it my love? I kept humming the gentle melody, and Sir Hemsley asked to be excused because it was causing him to nod off to sleep.

"I beg, Ahhhhhhhuuuummmm… Princess, please might I be excused; I am so sleepy." He yawned once more, and smiled with soft eyes that drooped over the bags beneath them.

"You may be excused Sir Hemsley, we shall get an early start shall we not? I asked to make sure he did not sleep too heavily and cause us to waste more time, we had done that way too much already in this chapter of our journey.

"Thank you Princess." He said as he bowed before me and backed out of mine and Sir William's sight and wondered off into the night towards his shelter leaving myself and my love all alone at last, and I was relieved, and kept talking even though Willy was now beginning to get bored, but listened with such strength of happiness on the outside, but I did not know his thoughts, I could only imagine what he was thinking.

"Music touches my spirit so, and makes me laugh and cry sometimes, but gives me much comfort; the Celtic music especially the violin is my favorite, it gives me good dreams, if not for reality, but fantasy and another world to dwell in for a short time. Sometimes I don't want to leave it... rebirth begins, and the light it brings from the dark beings with it much beauty. I always try to be definite with positive thought, and let all of the truth come forth even in such fantasy of dreams, there is an underlying truth to these dreams. This manner of thinking enables us to heal our insides from past pains that we have experienced; that my love is a part of assurance that we have true friends, and true love... Does it not?" I Asked William so he would not fall asleep whilst I was talking like a true woman does... constantly, but needed feedback on top of it all so I could continue knowing that he was really listening to what I was saying.

"I, I, why yes it does my love, it surely does." He yawned and I continued my thoughts, although I was exhausted, I just could not sleep this night and not for the lack there of it, but because I was wired for sound and needed to let my inward spirit flow like streams and waterfalls from the meadow that lay beyond my mind's eye.

"If someone removes this velum from me I would be paranoid about life, but this concealment of protection that is over my head clothes me as if it were a fisherman's netting, and it seems as though it is trying to be pulled away from me so to expose what lies beneath my sanctity of sanity leaving the membrane of young mushroom to act like a curtain covering its stalk and cap of immaturity, and it seems to be rupturing as the mushroom matures, leaving remnants at the base of the stalk, and some tissue flecks at the crown of the cap. Why is this so my dear William, please tell me my love, why?" I laid my head in his lap waiting for his answer to come, but he dozed off to the wails of the night wind.

I too pitched a mournful cry as if sirens wailed from beyond the cliffs of Dover near my beloved Alexandria.

I shook William and he awoke suddenly with a jerking motion.

"Ahhh ahhh huuumm, yes that is so, but I too can not explain how it is you are feeling deep on the inside unless you tell me how it is you are feeling my love." He had to say something as he yawned once again and glanced down at my face and smiled.

"You do like all that I am telling you, do you not?" I was having some doubt that he was not totally listening, but it really did not matter, because I just wanted him to at least listen a little, and besides, I love to talk when given the opportunity to do so.

"Now where was I, oh yea; I enjoy this journey in all of its glory, the good, the bad, and the ugly with the beauty, and with time it brings to me such a thrill and lessons in life well learned. I want to savor life in all of its glorious flavors like ripened fruits and roasted meats over the open fire pit of life. My Mother Nature still is the elusive winner on many levels, and I savor her the most. Do you not savor her too my love?" I had to keep William awake so I would not seem so all alone in this strange land of many wicked things such as Ogre, Trolls, and other creepy things that go bump in the night.

"Yes; Yvonne my dear, you are so right in all your wisdom and you help me grow stronger with every word you speak to my sensitive ears." My sweet wet Willy was now totally awake once more, and looked at my inward child and youthful face with droopy eye lids, but could not now sleep any longer himself, and I knew that he would answer any question I asked of him as well as to give me his full attention now once and for all.

"The yin to the yang which is my significant other and somewhat better half in as much as it could be said; yes without a doubt it is you who completes me, and I shall not in this life or the next let you be extracted from me by anything or anyone. As I study the verses of the old and the new, I see the answers that are changing me for the better, and all who surrounds me is also changed for the better; are they not?" I only gave William a small chance to speak.

"Yes," He barely muttered his word with the slightest twitch of a wrinkled eye brow.

I continued to talk over and above anything he might eventually try to say, and it did not matter what he said, because I was not completely satisfied until I got out all of my thoughts, and there was not a single solitary thing he could do about it either, because I was the one on control and not him, nor Sir Hemsley, or anyone else as far as that went, and he knew it as much as I did, because I was the Princess, and ruler over all in this entire kingdom, but needed to make my life truly complete in the face of all these wild thoughts that are interring my head all at once.

"William I want you to always be supportive to all that I say and do; and as this fantasy collides with reality… I am not alone; it becomes a new world of life giving forces, so I shall make it easy for all of us here; I have to just deal with others in a stern manner that is all as it is much easier if you are true to yourself and true to me your princess and lover, keeping in mind that I am still a child, and you must protect me as we will soon be in battle with the rage of not only Stella, and her dragon, but me and the rage that lay inside this mellow child; a child who needs and wants to discover as much as I can about all things especially myself." My question was sort of indirectly put, but William answered once more.

"Yes; my love; my beautiful Princess Yvonne… yes; it is without a doubt so and it is that you have spoken so it is that I shall always obey your every word and your lovable and léoflic (pleasant) command although we are lovers right now, as soon as this thing is finished and we are back we shall be wed, and I too wish to have some authority along with you too my love." He kept his words true and forth right to the grind stone of speech.

"I will see my Dear William, I shall see once all this is said and done how much power we shall share in this realm of our mind's eye that we seek to bring forth into a new dimension that we are dwelling in at this moment." My words were forth right as much as his were, but more powerful, because I was in charge and would always be in charge even after we were married providing we did not loose our battle to come.

Chapter 8
The Lair of Stella and the Black Dragon

Morning came faster than I thought, and I did not get any sleep, but I knew that Sir Hemsley got his needed sleep, and William took a few cat naps now and again wilst I was talking my little fool head off like most women do all the time.

As we walked over the high mountain plains and its beautiful meadow of different wild flowers, various trees, bushes and an abundance of wild life including many deer, elk, pheasant and quail in addition to so forth t all the beautiful birds... yes even those wild birds of prey, the falcon, hawk, eagle, and the wise old owl of hoot-hoot I so admire because of all their cunning strength and wisdom. It was a bright morning, the breeze filtered over us with such calm, but soothing to our spirits.

Each new day be an endowment; if I awake then there is a meaningful raison d'être meant for me that day by means of a true and real purpose filled with an overriding concern, and usually the interests of this my castle in the sky realm, that justifies a supporting and tactful action that might otherwise be considered reprehensible.

Each new sunshine brings a new challenge with it at the crack of dawn; the moistness on the ground, the blossoming of flowers; chirping of the flying fauna; the sound of the winds as they cool the warmth of the day as the sun gets higher in the sky and scorches our flesh... making it reddish in tone, and the rains as they drizzle down from Father Sky to the ground of my Mother Earth beneath my feet to make blossom of flora pleasant to the weary eyes and to air their fragrances to our sometimes snotty attitudes as well as to our nostrils.

These are there for our pleasure, and they are natural things, not that of some sort of witchery or black magic and the like.

They were created by some higher power than that which I have been so use to worshiping; yes I now know there is a true God, and will only use my witch powers to be exonerated of my evil step-sister Stella, her pet the Black Dragon, and put an end to the Black Death threat has befallen upon my people at the evil of Stella's black and demonic powers; once all of these things are clear, then and only then shall I give faith to God who created us all, but at the same time, it will be God who will direct my powers in the proper way and use them for good and not evil.

The way others feel are important to me, but I will still have to maintain my royal powers, and my witches powers in every day life as I see fit to use them, and all for the soul purpose of good and not the latter of evil.

I shall not put others before myself and to do so would be selfless, but would also be an act that brings inner joy from what others have to endure and go through in their own lives; although I am egotistical I shall change this as well, but in due process. These things are delicate in nature and take much time to change.

The mountain top was full of life, and as we walked onward to our destination I studied all of this land of many new wonders, and knew that all in all I had my work cut out for me in order to change and destroy what evil creatures that dwell below this highland and beyond.

"These mountains; I am very interested in them, and will make them a big part of my world when the time comes. I know this land is good, and will help my kingdom grow bigger than it already is; I shall control all that is in this high mountain plains and all that lay below it, and my evil step-sister, nor her pet the Black Dragon will spoil my quest. It is almost time for their doom my friends and I can feel the atmosphere and the foulness of the lair, and know that we are very close to it now." I kept my strength and composure but was exhausted from lack of sleep, but I just did not care about sleep until the end of Stella and the Dragon, and knew that this battle would be a fierce and maybe a long one.

"Princess, you are right, we are close, my nostrils burn from the sulfur in the air, it is indeed a foul tang." Sir Hemsley belched out in not such a blissful way as he rubbed his dead beat eyes and held his nose for a brief moment to rid it of the fetid odor.

As we sat down on some nearby rocks to catch our breath, I could sit in judgment with my ears pounding from the beat of some sort of flutter in the distance, and as I looked skyward I could make out the figure of a huge black spot in and it was getting closer. My observation was correct, it was a dragon headed our way, and coming in fast.

"Quickly, get behind these rocks and bushes so it will not spot us." I leaped behind them first, followed by William and then Sir Hemsley.

It was a huge green dragon, but somehow it did not look fierce at all for some distinct reason, but it was huge, and almost serpent like from the base of its body to its fancy looking head, and it almost looked as though it was smiling as it flew over our heads, and I seen it look down at me with its big yellow eyes, and I could almost swear it winked at me as though to say I am only looking for food, and not any human to kill and eat; and then it flew off towards the east where it had come from in the first place.

As I looked real hard, straining my tired eyes, I viewed it swoop down and pick up what appeared to be an elk with its big-sharp claws, it bellowed one last wail as the dragon went out of my observation.

"That was close Yvonne." William whispered as he wiped his brow.

"Yea my Princess, it was way too close for my comfort as well!" Hemsley loudly cried out as he too wiped his brow from fear.

"You two are supposed to be brave warriors, not little mice, or foul, are you not?" I let them have a piece of my mind with a slight snicker beneath my breath.

"Yea, that we are my Princess, we are men and not mice, nor foul as you have called us, and when the time comes we shall fight the beast with all our valor my Queen along with you Sir William who shall be King and Prince when all is said and done; then I will call you my King." Sir Hemsley stood erect before me and bowed with his sword drawn to his shoulder so to honor me and Sir William as commander, Princess and Prince; soon to be Queen and King of this domain and William followed suit with respect to my satisfaction, and I so enjoyed their seduction to my will, and was well pleased.

The sulfur of hot volcanic rock and lava kept getting stronger as we approached the honeycomb of caves that Stella and the Black Dragon proclaimed as their domain and soon to be fallen kingdom. There in the midst of a shadowed opening in a cliff was a vast cavern that was hallowed out eons ago with a division of geologic phases comprising two or more eras, and none quite as beautiful as I have ever seen coming from such terrain as what lay before my eyes.

We knew that we must exercise much caution to a ceaseless pounding beneath the domain of the volcanic activity with unpredictable and sudden violent outbursts to its temper ; we may have to escape its ooze of red hot candy from the caverns and shoots; it would be a dangerous venture beneath to where Stella had constructed her castle on the inside of the towering mountain of smoke, ash, flames, hot lava rock and on top of it all was the Black Dragon who in all its fury also had the ability to spew out flames that would devour any foe or idol threat in its path at its own will, and to me that was an even more dangerous threat than the volcano itself was.

Walking on the ground was difficult because of the slight heat that it generated, and I wondered how it was that my evil step-sister was able to withstand such warmness and such a foul stench as the sulfuric gasses it produced all the time.

One cavern lead into another and it was a maze beyond the mind's eye; the realm of a live volcano was breathtaking in the ways of both good and bad; with streams of bubbling lava surrounding us in every phase of our trip inward to the very pits of hell itself, but we kept on trekking deeper and downward to reach our goal; the lair of pure evil that we must destroy.

A cool breath of what was fresh mountain air hit my nostrils all of the sudden as we reached what seemed to be the last of the caverns, and as we came from behind the smoke filled areas to this cavern, it was way different than the others; it had walls constructed of green and blue Jade rocks, the air was livable, and as I rubbed my eyes to clear them of soot and sulfuric smoke, I beheld four figureheads of legendary winged beasts carved with the skill of a great craftsman, and I wondered who the carver was?

As I came closer to one of them; I could see Diamonds, Rubies, Safire's, and Emeralds embedded in the statues of these mythological beasts of long ago; they seemed to have been taken out of the early Roman Empire before my peoples time; and they were beautiful... beautiful enough to place in front of my castle back in Alexandria, and if I had my way about it they would also be mine as soon as I could take them from this dreaded place of kismet and rankle that makes one to become increasingly bitter, irritated, and resentful to the very cause that brought them to this my country.

I was in awe, but had more important things on my mind at this specific stage filled with the utmost of trouble and necessity at the same time.

Veins of flickering light as ruby ambers were coming from still another cavern above some ivory stairs, and I felt a presence of something wicked coming our way as did William and Sir Hemsley.

Quickly we fled back into the cavern that we had just came from so our human scent would not attract the nostrils of what ever it was that was headed our way.

We hid behind some smoke covered lava rocks that were singing my hair from its tremendous temperature, and I wanted so much to cool its burn down, but did not dare move a single solitary muscle, nor twitch even an eye brow lest we be seen.

My eyes almost popped out of my sockets when I seen a shadow of a long past demon figure of a woman walking and humming some sort of chant as she strolled by us. It was another mythological spell binder that could turn a person into stone if one was to look at her face; I forced myself to make my companions cover their eyes and not look at the monster Medusa who had hair made from serpents and a face like a thousand prunes.

Stella had powers stronger than I thought she had, and I knew that I would have more than my hands full now since I seen her array of demonic friends that dwelt in her company. I had to use my charisma and spell binding powers to captivate these beasts somehow, and knew that I needed a real strong spell to charm Medusa with; I knew her powers and mine had to be stronger so I would not turn to stone, but was there such a spell in my Book of Shadows to help me, because in order to turn her into stone from her own image, I needed a special reflective spell, and I had no mirror to make her see her own image with.

"Thank God this evil woman has passed us by." I told William and Hemsley as the sweat ran down my face causing me to wipian it from my brow with long light strokes of relief.

"What was it Yvonne? I did not se it." William exaggerated his words as we came from behind the rocks and back into the clear cavern where the figureheads were posted below the stairs.

"You would not have wanted to see that evil one Sir Will, nor you Sir Hemsley lest you wanted to be turned into stone for all eternity." I wipianed my brow once again and coughed for some needed fresh air.

"The Greek mythological creature is said to be an evil guardian of the caves in which she died; Medusa (Μέδουσα) the gorgon; the chthonic underworld female monster is said to cause all who look upon her hideous head turn to stone; it is here that in ancient tomes she roamed and her spirit is said to still dwell in these caverns; her head had been severed and placed here, it is said to have a hundred snakes as her hair that flicker about in random haphazardly motions, and the monsters eyes have fire inside of them as if they were the volcano's hot lava that turns one to stone." I explained to Sir Hemsley and my betroth Sir William what had been told to me by my dearly departed father Prince Zelstar; I continued as the hideous monster went out of my view.

"How awful Princess" Hemsley interrupted Princess Yvonne's train of thought.

"Please let me continue my tale; as I was about to say…this underworld of evil had been linked to describing all women as monsters; a gorgon's abilities connote and imply a consequence of malevolence; despite her once being an original beauty, her name came to mean monster woman, a idiom of which we use in other words right here in this mythical realm. When it is ask of a woman what be her rage; she most always says that they call her a Medusa; or the snaky-haired monster of a woman or the most horrifying woman in the whole world? I for one appose and despise such turn of phrase; if a gorgon be this horrible that she can turn a human to stone; then she be the more powerful of all witches in this realm of the insane; when the image of this sort of monster be a chart to all that lie within us all through our terrors and the depths of our anger into the resources of our own power as a women, and we misuse our power and make it evil as this Medusa monster had become, then we too are monsters in every sense of the word within ourselves in view of the world about us." Yvonne so often became long winded just to make a mediocre argument in spite of what others may be thinking. This is just how she was at times like these; she concluded her long winded puffs of nonessential craziness to the situation simply because she was on edge like most women so often get in stressful times.

I sat down beside one of the stone figureheads of antiquity and began to search through the Book of Shadows for a spell that would protect me from being turned into stone from the snaky haired monster - Medusa ; it appeared to be an easy spell, so I cast it on myself and cast a protective spell on William and Sir Hemsley and then began to search for a spell to turn something into a mirror so the beast would see her own image and turn herself into stone for eternity, but there was none to be found in the Book of Shadows.

I thought and thought for some time, and it came to me that I would just have to place myself before a reflective pool of liquid and expose myself before Medusa so she would draw near enough to me to force me to look at her ugliness, but I would not be able to see her because of the spell I had cast upon myself, but I was not going to take a chance and confront her face to face, but by looking into a pool and see my own reflection and her to see only her own reflection. It would be a clever trick if only I could find a good enough pool and lure her before it, that would be the hard part, because if something went wrong with my spell, then I would be doomed to face being stone myself for eternity and not her; I had to devise a good plan for this one, and ask my companions for their advice of trickery and cunning so I would not run my mind's eye into the ground with worry and the like because it would make me a wee bit trifle with a small amount of significance, and value if I could not come up with a good enough plan, and besides it would make these two men think for once and not play lame as most men are.

"Sir Hemsley, are you a clever person?" I asked with authority looking him directly in his reddened eyes.

"I, my lady, that I am. What is it you wish of me my Princess?" He stood up with a curious wonder on his face and bowed to my authority like a good warrior and servant to my royalty should do.

I knew he was not too bright, but ask him any way.

"How would you lure that mythical creature safely to a clear pool so she could turn herself into stone?" I was direct and did cut right to the chase without pussy-footing around about the matter.

"I am not so sure my Princess, and beg your forgiveness because I will just have to think about this one for awhile if you would like me too." He was so unsure of himself at that moment and scratched his head viperously several times and walked away in a bit of shame, but with a little humility to save face before myself and Sir Hemsley of Wales.

"And you, my Dear William, are you clever enough to devise a good plan to lure this beast to her stony statuesque demise?" I smiled at him because he was way more intelligent than Sir Hemsley and might have enough cunning to come up with a plan, but he too was not so sure about how to do it.

"Yvonne, I beg of you my love, I too will have to give this some thought. Will you do the same, and maybe we can all search our mind's eyes and put our heads together on this one my wife and queen to be." William always had a way with his words that made me iswowen with happiness, excitement, adoration, and infatuation.

"Very well, we shall all have to use our heads and devise a good plan to kill this freak of a body-less woman with the snaky hair Medusa must reflect her own image in a pool, but where in this place shall we find such a pool?" I thought and thought as did William and Hemsley.

Nothing was clever enough at that moment, so we moved onward and began to climb the ivory staircase that round with such twists and turns as they made a surge from the stem with a sourdre from below to the height of the cavern that they were beginning to make me a little faint.

Soon we were at the pinnacle of the swirling staircase, and I sure was relieved when we finally got there because it seemed to take forever and my legs were as a soft leather strap attached to my undergarments; setting down on the step I felt as though I was at a point of admitting stupian, but did not blurt out any words of defeat.

"I will not bow to your will Stella, no matter what evil magic you try to put me through; is that clear? Do you hear me? It is I your one time step-sister Yvonne and I have come to rid you and your Black Dragon from trying to destroy me and my people." I shouted at the top of my lungs.

"Are you alright Princess? You startled me so!" Sir Hemsley almost jumped out of his flesh, even as bulky as he was.

"Yvonne, why did you shout so, and with such fearful words in your pitch. It is not in your character to do such things my love!" William exhausted himself with much worry in his face.

He knew I was under a lot of pressure, but did not realize just how much pressure I really was under.

"I, I am adequate enough in my manner my love, but have heard my evil step-sisters voice in my mind's eye. She is nearer than we realize; we must exercise great caution from here on out; her evil creatures are all around us and at play; this is my evil step-sisters realm, and their playing field that we trod upon and we may not know when they will move quickly in on us." My mind raced with thoughts of death, for it lurked near and afar as well.

While setting at the top of the staircase; just in front of a huge doorway; I could hear chatter and hostile utterance coming from behind it. It was Stella's accent and I knew it, but said nothing to William and Hemsley, they would find out sooner or later what she sounded like, and what she looked like as well.

Stella was beautiful; more-so than I, and you could say I was a bit envious of her, but I warned William on that night we were in his hut back in Alexandria over two week previous to interring this evil terrain inside of the volcano of evil, and the place where the foulest, most vulgar, obscene, offensive and expressive behavior in witchery was set in motion for all dramatis personae of this stage were at the alert for the most harsh of critique for those who enter this world of prose, wording, and sheik design that even an old man in his mid fifties as my dearly departed father Zelstar would be well pleased with, let alone my mother and myself who has one of the most unique characters in literary intelligence, wisdom, sarcastic astuteness in the utmost feel of being clever and perceptive in aptitude.

Yea; I know that I am on a bit of the shrewd and discerning side; especially where personal benefit is to be derived, but what more should one expect from such an awesome personality with distinct persona and behavior in literary character of a Princess such as I portray before all of my subjects in this my world of daydream and fancy that is laid out on such a festive plate to be devoured by those who wish to partake there-in of its delicacies.

I knew that we needed a protection spell before we all made our way into Stella's world, so I opened the Book of Shadows with just one wave of my hand, and the Wall of Fiery Protection spell swished itself before my eyes.

I could see that it was going to take a little bit of preparation, and I had to conjure up some of the needed materials for the spell as well because I had not enough room, nor time to pack such luxuries for this my quest to end the evil powers of Stella and destructive forces of her Black Dragon.

As I looked at the spell and then at my companions, they ask me to read it to them so that they would have an understanding of what I had to go through as a powerful sorceress of witchcraft and I obliged then by doing so with empathy.

"Ahummm, very well." I began. "I shall read it all to you my friends, and pray you will not ask such a thing of me again; ahummmmm." I sighed with an easy tension of attitude.

Wall of Fiery Protection One Spell

"It says here:" I cut my long winded speech a tad shorter then usual.

"This is the best answer to any malicious spell directed against you and those you love and care about; it puts up a powerful protection against other witches who are jealous rivals, but will not create harm; it only gives protection whilst I am conversing with my evil step-sister Stella; I will be able to keep my karma pure, and yours as well." I smiled and continued. "I shall need the following items." Yvonne's eyes protruded from their sockets as she read the list and its contents.

What Ye Shall Need

7 Purple Offertory Candles
1 Black Offertory Candle
1 White Cross Candle
1 Bottle Fiery Wall of Protection Dressing Oil
1 Packet Fiery Wall of Protection Powder
1 Packet Fiery Wall of Protection Incense Powder
1 Packet Fiery Wall of Protection Mineral Crystals
1 Saint Michael Archangel Holy Card
1 Packet full of Graveyard Dirt
1 Whole Angelica Root

This will not be all you will need for this spell, look for this as well as part of your preparation...In addition to these things before your eyes, ye will need a clean white square of cloth, a small square of tin, scribe your rivals full name nine times on a small piece of clean scroll tablet; if his or her name is unknown to you, write 'The One Who Is Evil' nine times on the scroll tablet."

As hard as it was, I used my powers to conjure with allot of agile hand movements and access all that I needed for this long and painstaking spell, but it would be well worth doing it.

Now you are ready to set in motion the spell Wall of Fiery Protection.

Cones on an incense on a burner shall thou make the Fiery Wall of Protection of Incense Powders into.

The Graveyard Dirt must be placed in a China-Ware Saucer."

This one made me mad enough to spit coffin nails at the Book of Shadows.

"Damn it, now I have to stop this spell and make this object before I continue." My nostrils wanted to breathe flames fire like that of the Dragon as my mind began to burn with its fire.

"What is it you need Princess." Sir Hemsley asked with a half assed smile on his bulky puss face.

"Damn it, I need this china-ware saucer that the spell calls for." I glanced at him as though I wanted to devour him, and gave him a smeirwan of all smirks of a half assed smile right back that expressed feelings of my superiority, self-satisfaction-O, and conceit inside my insolent smile.

"I beg Princess, if you please, be ye patient, and I sill look inside of my pack; I believe I have such a ware for you my Queen to be." He tore into his pack and flung all of things in front of himself, and low and behold he actually had a china-ware saucer.

My eyes did not believe what they beheld, but I was ecstatic when I seen the saucer and grabbed it before he had a chance to say a word, let alone grab it himself, and I placed it before me and began to make the cones atop it. I smirked at him once more with a much friendlier one in appreciation for his good deed. He smiled back at me and William followed suit.

"Now where was I-ooooo?" Yvonne often used tidbits of African dialect filtering their way into her vocabulary from time to time, but she paid it not too much attention and proceeded with the spell of protection.

"Oh yes, here I am; now let me see-ooooo.

Prepare next the White Cross Candle for all who is to be protected. With a Coffin Nail ye must carve these words into it: Saint Michael Protect Me, William, and Sir Hemsley." I was puzzled once more, and did not make any coffin nails.

I began to cough from a dry throat and out came a shinny Coffin Nail; I gagged slightly as it came from my throat and landed on the step in front of my feet and almost rolled off to the stone floor that lay far below where I was sitting.

William reached down faster than lightning and grabbed it just in the nick of time.

"That was a close one." He exclaimed as he handed it to me and then proceeded to clean his fingers on his dull brownish-yellow color khakis woven from textiles ultimately from Persia.

"Dear William, you are always my life savor and I shall reward you greatly upon our return to Alexandria my love." I smiled and gave him a big kiss, coughed once more and then proceeded with the spell again. I then began to carve the candles as directed by the protection spell as well as follow the rest of the commandments.

"Put a coat of the Wall of Fiery Protection Dressing Oil onto the White Cross Candle

Take the Angelica Root and coat it with the Dressing Oil, and then put it in place at the foot of the White Cross Candle.

Make a circle from the Fiery Wall of Protection Sachet Powder around the centered White Cross Candle, and the Angelica Root"

"Wheeeeew, this is not an easy spell." I exclaimed as I wiped my brow of its sweat; since I be on pins and needles inside my mind's eye.

"Here Yvonne… take some water; it will help you somewhat in this awful heat." William gave me his deer skin pouch of Artesian Well Water to help with her dry heaves of thirst.

I took a huge drink to cool my throat that had been filled with the foul odors of sulfur, smoke, and volcanic soot, and then spat the foul dust, saliva and a tiny bit of blood out onto the ivory staircase and it made a black stain as soon as my spit landed on it; and I took still another small drink; wiping my mouth afterwards with the torn off sleeve of my brown and white deer skin dress.

"Thank you Dear William that was what I needed to cool this bad sensation in my mouth and throat."

I leaned over to him and gave him a kiss on his cheek and then proceeded with my spell.

"Seven are the Purple Guardian Candles… these ye must carve into them the names of seven saints, seven brave warriors, or seven family members… or a combination from these three entities; now prepare these and haste not. With the Fiery Wall of Protection Dressing Oil dress them now and place them on the circle just to the inside of the circle of Sachet Powder which flows around the White Cross Candle. Be careful while ye carve, and carve only one complete name in each White Cross Candle; it is important not to make mistakes with this one.

Sprinkle each Purple Guardian Offertory Candle with a smidgen of the Sachet Powder.

Place Saint Michael Archangel Holy Card in their midst.

Now take the Black Perpetrator's Candle and prepare it as your final step. With the Coffin

Nail, now carve your rivals full name, or the One who is Evil into it on one side and then the words 'Keep Away' on the opposite side. Warning… Do Not Dress This Candle, but instead leave it off to one side and outside of the circle of candles. Now on the pinnacle of the scroll place this candle, and put the saucer of Graveyard Dirt next to this Black Perpetrator's Candle.

Candles all… they must be lit from this order or ye shall be hit by your own doom. Exercise caution here as well fair witch.

First torch the Purple Guardian Offertory Candle.

Second torch the White protection Cross Candle within the circle.

Third torch the Black Perpetrators Offertory Candle well beyond the circle to its outside limit.

Fourth torch the Wall of Fiery Protection Incense Powder, and as it burns strong… say aloud your wish for protection praying and calling upon the Heaven for its share of provision to your aid.

Next ye must call upon Saint Michael the Archangel and ask him for his intercession for it is he who guards Heaven with his razor sword of two cutting edges… ye must enjoin with him in a secret pact and protect the ones who need protection along with the Seven Guardians as thy help-mates, and it does not matter if they be Guardian Angels or Human Guardians.

The Black Guardian Offertory Candle must burn to half of its length and then pick it up holding it in thy hand; now take the Name Scroll laying it on the saucer of Graveyard Dirt and then torch it with the perpetrators own Black Guardian Offertory Candle saying these words.

Your evil self shall be your own undoing! Let it be done now.

After the scroll had burnt to an ash, turn the Black Guardian Offertory Perpetrator's Candle upside down so to douse it in the Graveyard Dirt and say these words.

Your evil works shall be your ending! Let it be done now.

Ye must allow the rest of the Candles to burn until they douse themselves out.

The Angelica Root must be gathered up along with some Sachet Powder and the Saint Michael Archangel Holy Card; now place these in the tin and wrap them tightly to make a very minor sachet.

Next ye must tie the sachet inside the White Cloth by means of four knots.

Take some Wall of Fiery Protection Oil and dress it nimbly.

Place this on yourself for protection, but if ye have others with thee, then ye must make copy of it for each person and have them carry it with them as well for protection, and this same sachet is also useful to protect thy own dwelling place and when ye use it for dwelling protection, place it next to the door.

Ye have one final step and the protection spell shall be completed and all will be protected as long as it is carried on yourself at all times.

Ye must now make this place a clean environment, and when this is done, it shall rid thee of any other unclean rivals, foes, and predatory beast or creature that crosseth thy pathway.

All left over things including all melted Candle wax and the Coffin Nail; the Graveyard Dirt that is left on the China-Ware Saucer that contains the perpetrator's ashes; his or her doused Candle, and carry them to a graveyard and toss them hard against a grave stone and break the saucer at the same time you throw this muddle."

This spell was starting to get to my intelligence; it was one small setback after the other, and now I had to place another spell upon myself in order to vanish myself to a graveyard to throw this stuff against a grave stone, and them re-appear beck here as fast as I left this God awful and unholy place.

I finished reading the spell before I done this course of action that I now had to deal with, but it too needed to be done if I was to succeed in my witchery and cast the perfect spell from my awesome Book of Shadows.

"Warning… Ye must turn away and walk away… do not say a word and do not look back upon it.

Now take this final step… put all of the remaining things away and clean up with some clear Clean Spring Water, but you must first dissolve the Wall of Fiery Protection Crystals in the water as a floor purifier, and then wash thy hands with the same solution to purify them while at the same time ye recite the Thirty-Seventh Psalm: "Thyself shall fret not with evil doers" say this thirty-Seven times. Ye can also use this in your bath as often as ye wish too."

I had one final dilemma, and that was, now I had to say still another spell to draw and fetch a pail of clear clean spring water to clean up my mess, and this irritated me to no limit, but I knew that I must finish my work and clean up after myself like any good child must do.

I said the water fetching spell and then completed the protection spell at last… thank Heaven and God, but I was also tired and needed rest, but could not rest in the place and position that I was in at this time, and I sighed ever so slightly beneath my breath for some needed relief.

"The spell is cast, and now is the time for me to confront Stella my evil step-sister." I stood up with all the confidence in the world and faced the door.

"Are you sure we are all protected my lady." Sir Hemsley had some doubt on his face, but I reassured him that all was well and that we would all be protected from her powers.

"All are now protected and you have nothing to fear but the word fear itself rest assure my friends." My confidence grew stronger as I placed my hand on the door bolt at the ready to open it. I knew that it had been a long time since I talked with, or confronted Stella, but it had to be done again right now, and right this moment.

"Sir Hemsley my friend you stand at the ready on the left of the door with sword drawn, and William, you stand on the right holding the door open for me your Queen, and you have your sword drawn at the ready as well, and I shall stand my ground in front of the open door and talk to her without reason and try my best to force her to surrender before she is destroyed; that is very doubtful, but I must try. One more thing and this is a strong command to you both… Do not under any circumstances look inside is that absolutely clear. You must look outward until I command you to do so otherwise." I meant every word, and they knew it too.

"Yes, my lady." They both said at the same time and waited for me to pull the door completely open.

As I opened the door I seen the backside of the monster Medusa; the snaky hair was swaying in all directions and the serpents rattled and their tongue's hissed fiercely at the slightest of movement. She stepped to one side, and there stood Stella, and she had not been turned to stone like all the others who have confronted this monster Medusa; I turned around and faced the ivory steps, and they shown my reflection in them.

"Do not look at her lest ye be turned to stone, stand completely still and you will not be harmed, do not say a word; I command this of you now. Stay as still as you possibly can."

Medusa came toward the door like the slithering snake she was and as she reached the doorway she bent forward to try and grab me, and saw her own reflection in the still wet ivory stairs before she took a hand hold of me; and then it happened; she turned herself into a stone statue like she had done to so many other mortals in all her days.

She would now never stone another human being in all of eternity, for herself through my protection spell she done in her own evil and a stone death was her final fate.

Stella looked at the monster Medusa who was now her own gravestone monument and did not believe what her eyes beheld before them.

"Yvonne my onetime step-sister… my how you have became such a beautiful witch." Stella had not changed in all these years; she was just as crude and sinister in her mannerism as she had always been.

"Yes it is I Princess Yvonne, your master now Stella. You must surrender to my will now you evil bitch witch." My words were meant to be as harsh as I could possibly make them to be so Stella would understand that it was I and not her who were in control now.

"How dare you speak to me in this childish behavior? Do you know who you are dealing with? It is you who is the bitch witch and not I… Yvonne." Stella said with evil intensions in her articulation. Her aurora glowed as she spoke, and it burned with red, and yellow flames as though she was ablaze from stem to stern, top to bottom, for and aft all at the same phase. Her stage of development was clearly distinguishable and a sequence of events was forming inside of her pose, and what a beautiful physical painting she was, and I was jealous of her beauty, and that angered me all the more.

She waved her hands twice, stopped and waved them twice again; casting one of her evil spells toward me, but it did not phase me in the least.

"Hahahahahaha." I laughed vigorously at her. "Stella, Stella oh dear evil Stella; have you lost your witches touch my dear." I said as I laughed at her once more, and cast a Be Naked Spell at her.

"Hahahahaha… you have no power over me, take a look at yourself O-Evil one." I stood my ground and just smiled at her as she looked at herself being unclothed before me.

"Sir Hemsley and Sir William, may I introduce my evil step sister Stella to you now." I said to my two warriors and companions, and they came from behind the door, and seen Stella naked on all of her shame and glory.

"She has no clothing on Princess." Sir Hemsley said and covered his eyes and turned his back on her in a helter-skelter sort of way.

"How dare you Yvonne! Shame me in front of men; how dare you!" She waved her hands in a frantic motion and re-clothed herself once more with black adornment and bangles made of precious jewels, and vanished herself from our presence in shame and embarrassment.

William joined me in laughing, but had eyes as big as pieces of gold shillings. His face was as red as a freshly cut beet set before me on a silver platter and ready to eat.

"Yvonne, your Angeland Witches cræft is very powerful! Please, I beg, my gut is busting with hilarity at such a sight as what you have just performed before my eyes… HAHAHAHAHAHA." He almost fell onto the floor with laughter and had Nile crocodile tears streaming from his blue eyes so hard it blurred his vision, and when he reached towards me to hold me, he stumbled over the tail of Medusa, and took a look at her stone image for the first time, but did not turn to stone, because he was protected from my protection spell.

"Sir Hemsley, she has vanished and you can uncover your face now." I giggled at him with my childishness, and all he done was smile from behind his red face.

Princess you are indeed toe most powerful witch in existence that is one thing for certain." Sir Hemsley looked at Medusa's stone image and turned away just like William had done, because of her ugliness, and he too did not turn to stone, because he had a magic protection sachet in his pocket like I and William had, and was protected from all evil as well.

We walked into the room where Stella had been, and it was a great cavern inlaid with shinny green jaded stone, and had lots of furnishings of wealth and luxury that she had conjured up or stolen one from some place in this kingdom or perhaps a kingdom of some poor unfortunate soul of a ruler or two over the years since she was vanished from Alexandria by our mother the great Shauna who was the Mother of all great witches of all times.

My powers and Stella's combined would not equal her powers, but mine were more close to my mothers than my evil step-sister Stella's was; even though she was just a little older than I.

"Will you look at this place? Is it not a sight to behold?" Sir Hemsley was amazed by all the fancy things inside this awful place that Stella had made into her home.

"My castle Davenport is much better than this place, but all of this shall be mine now as well once Stella is out of my hair once and for all." I looked everything over with much curiosity, and as I did, I could hear Stella still complaining how much I had embarrassed her before my two men companions, and I could not help myself but laugh some more from time to time.

"Yvonne." William said as he picked up an amulet of some sort. "What do you think Stella will do now that she knows she is no match for you?" He looked me square in the eyes his eyes from side to side looking for my evil step-sister Stella to re-appear with some other creature or even the Black Dragon by her side.

I could tell that both he and Sir Hemsley was uneasy and on their guard at all times, but ready for a fight if one was to come about.

In the distance we could hear the fierce roars of what could be several dragons bellowing different pitches all at the same time. We walked back out the door, and the roaring got somewhat louder, and was coming from another cavern far below our position atop the swiveling ivory staircase.

I dreaded the long winding trek back down the staircase, but this had to be done. I had to re-locate Stella and her demon the Black Dragon and maybe several other dragons as well; after all when we were outside, a green dragon appeared overhead in search of food, and had carried off a big Bull Elk for its lunch.

Soon we were back down the winding staircase of ivory, but now the hard part of searching through all these many caverns of sweltering rocks, volcanic emission pools, smolder, and vapor's of steam. One cavern fed into another; and as we went deeper and deeper inside the volcano, I felt that we were forlorn with desperation and doomed to failure in its contents for all perpetuity.

My mind raced in and out as we made our way about the horrible place of evil and death, even though I knew we were protected from many things, but the volcano itself would not give way to any mortal nor witch no matter how much power one had inside of their being; this was a part of Mother Earth, and one thing that humankind would not be able to place any kind of spell upon no matter how hard one tried; it just could not be done, and I knew it deep down on my insides with such a gut feeling that it hurt so on my insides as well as hurting on the outside from all the misery of heat, soot, smoke and the smolder of sweltering rocks.

I began to shed some of my clothing so I could dry the sweat from my hot body, and soon I was down to most of my bare essentials exposing as little of my private areas as possible, but I knew it was driving William hotter on his inside more so than the heat from just the volcano itself.

As we approached another segment of the caverns realm I heard faint roaring that echoed through-out and penetrated my ears and entered my brain like a joyful noise of many thousand trumpets blowing in the canyons of my mind's eye.

I felt that we were near to where the Dragon was at least, but maybe Stella had just laid a trap for me and my companions with her magic; after all I did make her embarrassed when I cast a naked spell upon her atop the ivory staircase and I knew she was furious about me destroying one of her evil friends that she had conjured up from out of the past geologic era of time composed of several periods where-by all things, even dragons and devil like creatures had descended from when they were cast aside from the heavens because of trying to control all of its existence and beyond for eternity.

Stella was a cunning witch in her own right, but I knew how evil she could be when all odds were against her; I had to prepare myself for battle now for the reason that surely she had cast upon herself some revenge spells that I knew would work against mine; and it was highly unlikely that my protection spell would not be as strong as it should be, so I had to stop and think about what sorts of spells she might be able to cast against me and my comrades in arms causing us to sustain some sort of damage in our mortal flesh; and mortal mind's eye.

If I was to succeed in my quest here, it would be inevitable and impossible to avoid or to prevent an all out war from happening of not only witchcraft, but actual fighting as well.

"Sir Hemsley you must be prepared for a fight to the finish, be it yours, the dragon or even a fight to the death in hand to hand combat with my evil step-sister Stella; and William my love… you must also be at the ready for the same thing, but all in all you two must slay the Black Dragon at any cost; is this clear to the both of you?" I did not flinch, not even an eyebrow as I stood firm in my command, nor did I crack the slightest hint of a smile. My words were more serious than they usually were, and they knew I meant every word of all I said to them both.

"Yes my Princess, it is oh so very clear indeed." Sir Hemsley stood as straight as an oak tree as he spoke; not one brow did he flinch either as he drew his sword and shuffled his beady eyes to and fro on the lookout for any sort of danger that may be lurking near by us.

"Yes Yvonne my love, I shall fight her if the need should arise, but my first duty is to protect you the one I love from any and all danger, and I shall not ask permission from you do what ever it takes to ensure your safety and our success to slay the Black Dragon and help do away with your evil step-sister Stella the bitch witch of the east; and we must help all of our people by creating a cure for the Black Death that is upon them." William stood firm and with a high degree of dignity and total love and respect for not only me, but himself and Sir Hemsley; his eyes also moved vigorously to and fro in search of danger, and his sword was drawn and at the ready for a brutal crusade.

Chapter 9
Into the Dragon's Lair

There are battles, and then there are unique battles; this one would be an exception to the rules of normal warfare; we were about to embark upon the mother of all fights; not only because it would have witchcraft involved, but a fierce beast in that of a demon Black Dragon

As we approached the lair where a huge metal fencing was strung across one cavern sector to another with a huge lock in place at its center; I could hear heavy footsteps that shook the earth beneath my feet, along with a very familiar voice yelling a command that would curl a persons blood making it boil as though the very pits of Hell was about to erupt and collapse under tremendous stress and strain upon us all.

Stella's voice was harsh; her words extra nasty more-so than any one person that I had ever heard in their evil demands; and her look was just as wicked as her tone.

"Come on You Black Dragon Bastard; Damned you, what the Hell did you do to the Green Dragon's yearling? I wanted to raise this one and train it like I had done with you. I should beat out what little brains you have left in your beastly looking head." Stella had a hickory stick in her hand and hitting the beast as hard as she could, and it bellowed a loud roar that shook the cavern walls. And then she yelled at it once more with one final blow, and the beast roared even louder than before. "But I will leave that tiny bit of brains intact in your ugly pea brain head for now; you had best behave yourself is that clear?" She followed through with one last swat on his nose for extra measures; and then before she headed off to another cavern she yelled at it with a strong commandment.

"Get in your cage you Black ass demon until I am ready for you to destroy my bitch step-sister Yvonne and her scrawny little human companions she calls men; huh... so she thinks they are, but they are nothing that even I can't slay in a heart beat." Her words was foul and I kept hidden as much as possible behind a rock so she, nor the Black Dragon could see me, but I knew the beast sensed me and my companions hiding around the corner from its position as it glanced straight at me before it interred its confinement behind bars and padlock.

I took a fleeting look around one corner of the cavern wall as she disappeared behind a huge monolith and some stalactites... low and behold I saw the demon for the very first time up close. Its eyes were bright yellow, like that of a venomous serpent, the pupils were like coal, with a streak of red smack dab in the middle, and I could sense its power, but at the hands of Stella it seamed almost like a domesticated hound instead of a fierce demon dragon. Its face was harsh like a Gila monster with a large brightly colored venomous mouth that could devour any small animal or human if given an opportunity to do so, but most of these lizard monsters feed on eggs most of the time, but also have apatite's for and small mammals as well; and since this was more than a Gila monster type lizard; it was more on the side of a Godzilla creature with huge wings and a coal black body to match its head and other body parts than the normal Gila monster lizard or snake like Dragon was.

I looked down at its scaly legs and then at its claws; they were made of case hardened steel like that of a well made sword that could cut through almost any type of flesh as though it was cutting through goats butter and cheese to create a appetizer before the main meal was served, and I prayed that we would not end up beneath then and the beast for its nibble of an appetizer.

I knew by her tone and its evil look that they were both ready to fight to the finish without even eating any spinach, I kept a civil tongue in my mouth so not to expose our position to Stella and her beast of a lizard with wings that wanted to eat me like a tender steak before it went to bed.

We slithered back as quiet as we could to a much safer area and rested until daybreak the next morning.

I could not sleep very well, but at least I got some rest and arose early to shake Sir Hemsley and slap Sir William on his ass to awaken them so they could prepare themselves for battle with the demon Black Dragon.

"Get your lazy Asses up now, we must do what we come to do. Come-on gets a move on now time is of the essence and a demon Dragon waits its slaying and so does my mean immoral step-sister Stella." I rubbed my eyes with my hand and then leaned forward toward William and planted a big kiss on his lips… you might say it was one hell of a lip lock and I almost did not let go, but I pulled away before he had a chance to place his hands on my sensitive areas, and cause me to sway in fancy of sexual play instead of battle.

"Princess, are we not going to eat before we slay the beast my lady." Sir Hemsley said as he held his stomach like a little boy who had not eaten for a whole day.

"Yes, I too am a little hungry Yvonne my love, and that Kiss just wet my apatite for more than food." Willy seemed always ready for making love, but held himself the best he could.

"Later; when the beast and Stella are out of our way, I will be all yours, but for now we must feed our bellies." (Grrrrrrrrrr) My stomach rumbled and the two big boys laughed because of hearing it growl like an angry dog what was rabid and foaming at the mouth.

In all the life where-by the deity of witchery is brought forth into this realm of narrative characters there are none more cunning than I; yes I… Princess Yvonne of the Castle Davenport who has all the power to turn a beast into nothing more than a mere fly if I wanted to, and turn anything as far as that goes into what ever I so choose with my ingenious and artistic language, vocabulary, prose, and style of the mind's eye. With this in thought… I shall use all of this my power that my creator gave to me in order to rid myself, my companions and my people of Stella, but I know that it will take time to achieve the final end where-by my ultimate goal is met its match in this my quest of freedom in such a way that it shall set me loose upon this society and these creatures I shall call the so called human race.

Yes I Princess Yvonne shall also rid us of all the evil that flows from these mountains and all of its beasts that dwell here-in; and my people shall be set free of the Bubonic Plague, this Black Death, this plight from an ancient time that fell in the midst of modern times such as these that I now live within, yes it is a famine not like the locus, frog, fly, and rats plagues, nor the plague of hail that fell from the sky as fire once done in ancient times, this one has always been from the start of time itself, but is only brought about with some evil person using witchery in an evil and undulated way… like that from a watery fire that flows as if it were a njele of an únj□ I□ tàwree (needle of an unholy tarweed)… like that witch spews out of the devil's mouth himself.

He that was once was amongst the stars in the heavens above, but had fallen from grace to Mother Earth to crawl upon the ground as a snake and had slithered back to Mother Earth straight from the lake of fire and brimstone that is called Hell where it now dwells and still causes its evil to befall upon the people of Mother Earth as if it were all the particles of sands right out of all the oceans of time and nature as well as all of the flames from the pits of hell as well.

It is the one famine that is so hard to get rid of that it takes an even stronger spell than what the Evil One come up with through the mind of Stella to spread amongst us with.

I will have to drain almost all of my powers in this battle for survival amongst the fittest of warriors that I have in my midst whom shall slay the demon Black Dragon, and then I shall use all this my powers upon that Evil devil - step-sister of mine… Stella.

It will be a pleasure to slay her myself with witchery that is drawn from evil and made good, and I shall rest with peace when the deed is done, this I vow.

I knew that I must njele (needle) her with a remark and a very cunning action that would be intended to tease in addition to provoking her in an informal behavior with a complimentary style and mannerism inside her neural for the sake of inundating and overwhelming her with a huge quantity of things that must be dealt with before she could deal with me and my superior, skillful and excellence of witchery so I can lure her away from the lair of the Black Dragon, and give my men the opportunity to be able to slay the beast once and for all.

I would have to first cast a spell so I could create misleading and deceptive images of unruly creatures in her path as she approached the lair, this would distract her just enough so she would have to use her witchery in order to get liberated from their presence. I must then summon a white Unicorn of purity to charge her and spear her with its horn right in her evil heart, and this would send her straight to the pits of Hell to join her Black demon Dragon and her mentor the devil himself, whom I know would not be pleased with her performance want so ever. One only knows what her finale fate would be; God rest her evil soul, but I knew deep down inside of my very own spirit that her soul would never rest, and have peace, because it would be tormented for all eternity and beyond that was one thing I was certain of in my mind's eye.

Spell of Lure and Doom to Draw Your Enemy Away

Ogre mage you have the spell where you are your life like shadow shall be here to do its magic.

I command and cast you now.

You are my enemies doom.

Ten meter tall with skin of green and shadow blue and hair as black as soot on the morning dew.

You must say these words as your enemy comes forth saying their name aloud, but unheard my your enemy as well as your made-up foe; and when your made-up foe in shadow form appears; it is important to follow this exactly, and if you do not; then they both will be able to attack you instead, so exercise much caution and do not be distracted away from this spell you are casting, or you might end up as dead as a door plate.

Clone others when Stella appears, do not fret, the enemy can not slay thee, for you are not in flesh, but in shadow only as is your clones.

Lure the enemy far away from this place so we shall pass in safety.

You have ability to use all your combat strength at will when confronted by your enemy, and even though ye are in shadow form, your blows shall cause damage to your enemy and draw blood.

You are the superior force in battle, and if ye must retreat use your gaseous form and vanish never to return.

Cast now and come forth I command it, so it is said, so it is done.

As soon as I cast the lure and doom spell a ten meter tall Ogre mage appeared and stood silent on wait just inside of the cavern before reaching the lair cavern that the Black Dragon was caged in.

My plan was working well, but the battle had not begun, and I did not know when or if Stella would ever return back to the lair this day or not to make check on her pet demon Dragon. I was growing impatient, but had to maintain my calmness so that William and Sir Hemsley would not think me a mad woman once again.

I had to bring forth other such phony creatures of shadow from my Book of Shadows to lure Stella away from the dragons resting place inside the huge barbed steel cage that kept it at bay.

We did not know if it was day or night inside the caverns of the Volcano or not, and the heat was unbearable at times, but since we had shed most of our clothing to help stay cool, the heat was not much of a hindrance any longer, and it seemed to me that we were all getting use to its sting and foul smell. I still had the sulfurous tang inside of my mouth; it was bitter, but also getting to be bearable enough not to bother me and my warrior companions.

Stella soon came back several hours later with a basket of foul smelling morsels to feed her pet with, but as she approached the entryway to where Black was; she almost jumped out of her own skin, and I had to hold myself so I would not laugh out loud, but my insides hurt from the hilarity of her being so startled when she saw the Ogre mage blocking her way.

It snarled at her, and took several swings with its big spiked club; the basket that was in her hand flew to one side spewing out the freshly killed rodents that had been slightly cooked in hot volcanic lava just the way some dragons liked them before crunching every morsel even the bones would be devoured.

"What on Mother Earth, how did you get in here you big ugly Ogre mage, how dare you invade my domain? Be gone and be gone now I say. I command it this very day." Stella was in a rage, but the Ogre shadow did not budge. Her rage grew and this gave me opportunity to say the words the book said I should say to make other Ogre mage appear to chase and lure Stella away from the lair as I had planned.

Another Ogre appeared and then five more suddenly popped in on the unsuspecting Stella the wicked. I tried not to laugh, and it was hard not to it all inside of me, but I somehow managed to hold myself, and soon Stella ran off into another chamber screaming her fool head off.

"How dare you, go away you big ugly beasts, get out now, but they kept following Stella, and she had no idea that they were just false images that I had conjured up to make her flee so I and my companions could stand before the demon Black Dragon that held its ground behind the iron cage.

"Well - well, what do we have here, a funny looking Black Dragon". I said as I smiled at Sir Hemsley and my Dear William as they sort of hid behind my now skirted body that I quickly changed into with another magic spell when I was hidden, so that I would resemble Stella to the Dragon, and fool it into thinking I was her, and it seemed to be working.

My companions shook just a little in their boots, but also stood their ground.

"Do not make a sound". I said to the Dragon in a voice that also sounded like Stella "These mortals will not harm you, they only wanted to see what a real Dragon looked like up close and personal that's all my ugly black beast".

I shook my arm as though I had a whip in my hand, and made it appear to be so to the dragon. My plan was working like a charm, and the time was almost right for my men to slay the dragon, but how were they going to do it with the beast behind those iron bars.

I had to devise still a different plan that I knew would work in the long run, but what was it going to be.

I looked evil in the eye for the second time in my life, and it scared the shit right out of me, but I had to pretend so not to show just how frightened I really was.

"I must take these humans back to where they belong now, and soon my fiendish pet I shall fetch you a couple to feast upon, do not worry so damn hard about when alright you foul smelling monster". I knew I had to say something to the beast to make it think I was Stella, and walked away with my companion's right on my shirt tail.

We disappeared once more behind the rocks and back into the other chamber so I could come up with a different plan to slay the beast.

"Now we all know the size and strength of the dragon, and I must think of how we can slay this monster. Let's get out of here for awhile; I am getting way too hot in this miserable environment. We slowly made our way back out of the caverns of the volcano, and back out into fresh air. I know that William and Hemsley appreciated me wanting to leave that awful place to re-gather our thoughts and be able to breathe some proper air once again.

"Thank you Princess the fresh air is doing me some good, and soon I will be able to slay that monster, and what a monster it is, I know we will have a fierce battle to conduct when the time is right." Sir Hemsley wanted to continue his boastfulness but William butted in to stop his big mouth from continuing.

"Yes I too am relieved to be back out into the freshness of the outside, all of that volcanic gas was making me a little ill in my whole body". William stopped and excused himself so that he could stroll behind some near by bushes to take care of some urgent business.

Sir Hemsley followed and went behind a different set of bushes to relieve himself as well. I sat down on a nearby rock and began to devise a new plan, and as I did, I looked through the book of spells so I could cast still another spell upon Stella so she would not interfere too much, but knew that she would soon catch on to the trickery that I was playing upon her, and my battle with her would soon take place as well.

Unicorn Spell

Burning frankincense lay naked under a cloud of white where the purity of Unicorn play.

Unicorn horn heat the frankincense in the place where you play; and ruffle the fur; and poor out your magical white substance to make the valley below you raise to an all new height when the flame goes out.

The frankincense must be heated to its height at the same instance that the white substance flows forth in a volcanic magnitude and with all of your purple passion connected to the volcanic frankincense.

"What is this?" I shouted; "This spell is not right for some particular respect, but; ahhhhh… I know what spell this one is and it will also come in handy if truth be foretold soon." I chuckled slightly but did not reveal my powerful thoughts of deviousness to William and certainly not to sir Hemsley that was one thing for certain.

They both came back from beyond their private bushes and plopped their weary butts down on some near-by rocks.

I started to flip through the pages in a frantic; but laughed at the same time to throw my companions off their guard for the first time since we began this quest.

"Ahhhh… here it is, this spell is the right one." I said with s big smile and glared William in his beautiful and luscious eyes, and smiled with all means of a sinister and wicked woman with the ways of a whore. I wanted William so badly at that moment, but knew I must continue my spell casting.

Clearing my throat I started to say the proper spell at last, and knew that the other spell was placed before my eyes for a very good reason and a much more pleasurable use later.

I knew that William was as horny as I was, but we were on a very serious quest to free my people from the Black Death that had befallen upon my village some three hundred kilometers from our current location in the eastern sector of Angeland.

"Finally; here it is." I giggled like a girl on her first day of her witches education before a bunch of other witches and warlocks studying spells to be cast and making mistakes that were so often embarrassing to the student who made a friend into a frog of toad or some other misfortunate creature that had to plop around on the ground as though it was lost in a new world for the very first time and scared as stiff as a mans private parts.

Make a Witch as Pure as a White Unicorn

"To make a witch as pure as a white unicorn, you first need the following ingredients…

One sachet of Unicorn horn dust as white as the snows of a winter's mountain top.

One sachet of rose incense

One sachet of white cane sugar

One sachet of finely cut magic herbs selected for their specific spiritual powers.

Three stems from three pure white lilies.

Take the sachet of incense and heat it up with some rose colored incense and a little sugar for a bitter sweet potion.

Next add a small portion of the cut magic herbs for spiritual powers, and stir with the three pure white lily stems and say these words.

Purity, filled with sweetness and spiritual bliss, as this witch drinks this potion fills her with the purity of the white unicorn and give her the kiss of happiness to make her kind and gentle.

The witch whom this potion is to be given to must drink this in your presence, she friend or foe; it does not matter, it has to be drank in your presence, and you must drink some of the same, but it will not harm nor change you in any way, shape, or form."

"This spell is an easy one, but there is one problem, ic have to have Stella drink this in my presence and that is the hard part; how to do it without her casting a wicked spell upon me." Ich shook my head and rubbed my eyes in awe as to how ic would pull this one off without getting busted by my evil step-sister.

Ich thought and thought, and knew that in order for me to do this; Ich must change my whole appearance to someone whom Stella likes and trusts, but who… Ich knew no one who liked her except her dragon. I knew that I could not show my true self to her or she would know what ic was up too and do a real harsh number on me and then feed me to her evil pet Black Dragon for an appetizer and then feed William and Sir Hemsley to it as a main course.

"You do have a slight problem do you not my Princess". Sir Hemsley said with a slight sigh in his hard melodious throat.

"Yea, Ich do indeed have a major problem". Ic too sighed, and then ic knew that I had to do some real hard thinking back to a time when we were younger and playing together amongst our friends and think of who liked her best and that would be no easy task, but I had to do it none the less.

"Shall Ich go back to Alexandria and seek one of her friends for you my Princess"? Sir Hemsley smiled with a cheerful smile for the very first time that ic knew him. Hē was turning out to be a real nice man after all, even though he was a funny sort of bloke who liked other men instead of women. Ich shook at the very thought of his strange behavior but tried not to let on like his funny ways bothered me a lot.

"Thank you Sir Hemsley, but that will not be necessary, because it will take way too much time and that is something we have little of is time, and I want time to be on our side. Ich must think of who liked this bitch witch when we were younger that is all?" Ich smiled at him ever so slightly and gave a slow nod from my head for approval in a saddened sort of way, but approval even so.

Ich needed rest as night was falling upon us once again. It seemed like one thing after another was setting us back and out of reach of our goal and success in our quest to fix a very serious problem at hand to rid my people from the Black Death

As ic lay under a newly constructed sheltered structure that protects me and covers my frail but bosom structure and as it provided cover from the weather and nearby dangers it gave me a refuge and an establishment to also provide accommodations for my food. Ich need to leave the caverns of the volcano to a more open and less violent and otherwise dangerous situation of being so damn close to the demon, the beast with giant teeth that could chew me up like a tree branch and use my bones for its tooth picks.

The night air was cool and it sent shivers throughout my flesh and caused me to have millions of goose bumps in more than the usual places; they seemed to tingle me just a little between my legs and inside of my private area, and ic began to rub it a little; and it started to turn me on. Ich felt intense inside my hollow muscular organ in the pelvic cavity of my female domain, in which ic have been told that the fertility of a child is nourished and develops before birth.

The spiral tingles shook my insides with an ecstasy and it gave me vibrations of self pleasure that ic never thought ic would have or experience in my life, Ich love it when William makes love to me, but never knew that ic could pleasure myself in the almost exact same manner. After my ecstasy of self satisfaction to the sexual nature of my life, Ich lay there and rest for a short period while Hemsley snore away as if I was not even around.

I began to think and somehow William awoke and stair at me while I lay there naked as a jaybird atop my bedding and my breathing was slowly filtering down to a restful calm and I thought about this quest as well as other aspects of my life.

"Willy" Ich said as I looked at him looking at me; Ich am delicious about the process of sharing my friendship with you my love, and ic really love and appreciate all that you have done for me so far in our quest, but even more with all the wonderful love making you and ic have had since we came together back in Alexandria the day Ich summoned you, my prince Willy and the now departed Sir Clancy who suffered a horrible death shall rest in peace some where in time, this ic know, but we shall endure together for eternity together as one, this Ich am also sure of."

"Yes, my love that you are! You are very delicious in more than just that aspect this I do know." He smiled at me real big and ic smiled back at him with my eyes.

"Ich have no grievances with anyone else except Stella and my exchange of personal information is with you and you alone, so please if you have respect for me and love as much as you say, then ic plead with you this night, do not say a thing to Sir Hemsley and even after all is done here and our mission is completed no matter what the outcome, ic tell you do not tell another living soul as well is that clear my love."

"Yes Yvonne, I shall obey all that you tell me to obey and do, for it is to our advantage and our future together as husband and wife and our future children to come."

"How do you know that I am bearngebyrdu, (child-bearing, or with child); tell me this?" Yvonne was in awe to him knowing her secret of being bearnéacnigende (pregnant).

"I did not know Yvonne my love, but I say to you my princess. Are you pregnant and with child."

"Yea, that Ich am, and somehow ic too know that Ich am pregnant and with child it is yet to be determined, but ic recon that my body tells me Ich am is all Ich can figure out at this time, ic feel strange in the mornings, and my insides seem to be telling me that ic am." Ich (I) really did not know if ic was or not, but Ich said this to William so that he would fight even harder for me and not let me fall prey to the Black Dragon or my evil step-sister Stella.

Soon William was fast asleep once again as was Sir Hemsley, because they both snored like Wild Boar rooting in their own slop.

Ich (I) lay there thinking how ic (I) can be nasty or nice at the same time and still gossip, but it will always be about those ich do not like per say especially Stella, and so often ich do keep most things inside my mind for later use especially when one of my foes isn't around, or when Ich do not want even a friend to know my thoughts, because some of them seem to be able to read my mind if ich am way to close by them for some unknown reason to me, but as time goes by Ich shall come to know the reasons and figure out all things in life as ic should do to become an adult woman of full maturity and a ruler of mīn (my) kingdom as well as a mother my child and wife to my lover William.

As Ich (I) so often recall the early days of those relationships that ic once had with my now evil step-sister Stella, Ich start naming the likes and dislikes that ic learned about her especially those that ic had in common with her. They were more often likes and dislikes about either some sort of object, animal or person, not so much because of the once close relationship that ic had with that horrid person, that wicked step-sister of mine Stella, but more-so when the relationship was new and freshly placed before the both of us while at play either outside or in the confines of our rooms and the castle. Those likes and dislikes were treated as if we were identical twins or something, but knowing all too well that we were never twins, heaven forbid now; it makes me ill in my stomach every time ich think about it. But you know something? Now that ich think about all of this ic can use my memory recall to view the past and come up with a person that was really close to Stella and use all of these thoughts to my advantage and not hers.

As ich lay there on a pile of freshly cut grasses that was covered by one of our fur pelts. Ich recalled sharing a larger portion of negative interactions more-so than the positive interactions and attitudes and both seemed to be popping in and out of my mind like an ear of corn that had fallen into our open fire pit and began to pop and turn into a strange shape as well as becoming white in color and not yellow on its cob as it was at first; and as it popped it flew out in all directions. Ich did not know why, but Ich began to pick the strange popped corn up and eat them, and they were so tasty. This also gave me another one of my brilliant ideas that I could use as a weapon against Stella and her big ugly Black Dragon.

Mīn thoughts also flew in all directions like the popping corn in the fiery pit and it was a good feeling even though ic had a hard time sleeping, it gave me peace of mind to be able and find a solid solution to one of my many dilemmas of fighting Stella and her dragon.

Ich am going to place those positive thoughts into Stella's mind to help force her not to do so much evil against me and my companions so we can destroy the dragon and make her lift her evil spell of the Black Plague that she put upon my people. Ich really do not want to destroy her if ic can avoid it, but if it is down to push come shove; with all the force of being both rude and prehistoric like the Ogre's who dwell in this land of wickedness, desolation and destruction; Ich shall destroy Stella also.

Chapter 10
Prepare For Battle in Bedlam Bloke

Night sleep finally took its hand hold on my weary head, but I was restless with night thoughts about what was to come in the near future. Bedlam seemed to be grasping my brain with harsh intensity to a stimuli of insanity causing me to toss with a furious frenzy over the whole matter and when I awoke several hours later at the break of daylight; my head was all a-throb; like thunder it did pound, and my mind was my own asylum.

As soon as I arose I woke William and Hemsley.

"Wake up you two bloke's, soon there will be a battle and we must view it so we can gain knowledge on how we can defeat Stella and her evil Black Dragon." I shook both men as I talked in an authoritative voice.

"On this day when the battle shall begin; it will be a day when the evil Black Dragon shall fall along with my evil step-sister Stella; the two shall fight one another through my powerful spell that I will cast upon both of them with-out their knowledge whatsoever; it will be a glorious day indeed; but I also know that before that happens another mighty battle shall be fought outside the big cavern where they dwell; we shall make many throwing lances and arrows to use against the evil Black Dragon, but on this day I see two dragons fighting one another; a mighty female Green Dragon who is with young in her cavern den shall rise up against this Black dragon, and she will be hurt and flee back to her dwelling place to heal her wounds." My words rang true.

As soon as my vision has finished; the two dragons were fighting fiercely outside the big cavern and a young one looked onward to see if its mother would defeat the big Black Dragon or not.

We hid behind a different cavern wall looking onward; William and Sir Hemsley sure were anxious to fight, but since there were two dragons in the picture now they did not know what to do except look onward and see if my vision would come true further or not.

The two fought with all they had, and their blood spewed outward in all directions from the thrashing blows of their claws and huge sharp teeth that ripped deep into each others leathery outer flesh.

They dealt each other lots of collateral damage on the inside as well as outer damage, pain, and suffering was whaling its echo's back into the cavern and through-out the vast realm of the high mountainous lairs territory. Their mighty roars were loud, fire also flew from each others beastly jaws, and it was getting hotter by the moment; stalactites and malachite's along with cavern wall was torn down scattered like pebbles to and fro as they flew in all directions making it hard for me and my two companions to see the entire battle; but it was enough to know how much injuries the Black demon Dragon had sustained. We did not really care about the big green female dragon, because she had helped us in a long run that was one thing certain we could rely on in our diplomacy before we was to do battle with a wicked witch and a beastly dragon.

The mighty Black dragon walked away with a limp; scattering blood beneath it; the green dragon lay helplessly on the caverns messy battlefield. We were certain the female dragon was dead, so we walked out to see, but we exercised much caution in the slithery trek to where she lay upon the bloody cold battlefield ground.

As we approached its bloody body we could see breathing movement from its mighty chest; the blood slithered down scale after ridged scale; dripping onto the cave floor beside it and our feet. I felt remorseful. And carried a strong sense of guilt as well as regret for the beast, but at the same time I thought how I might help it recover so that it could live to fight still another day with other such beasts of disaster as she and the demon Black Dragon were.

I cast a spell of cures to heal its wounds; as I did I could swear that I heard it speak in a faint whisper to me; telling me much thanks for sparing her life, and that once she recovered and her wounds healed, she would help us even further to defeat both the Black demon dragon and evil Stella the wicked as well.

"Did you say something William?" I looked him square in his beautiful dark eyes and he into mine; and he replied me well.

"Neigh my Princess of love, that I did not say a word." He frowned with his bushy eyebrows and mouth in a downward manner. His tone was almost taking on the characteristic of a horse full of the sense of fear before it reared in protest to warn of an enemy.

"Sir Hemsley did you say something to me." He also frowned at me in the same surprising manner.

"Then if neither one of you said any thing to me, then who or what did." I looked down at the green dragon's large horned head and its eyes opened the fiery dense glow from her red eyes and they glanced up at me, and then gave me a wink along with what looked like a smile.

I smiled at it and then nodded my head as a good Princess should do for a well done approval of her fierce battle; and then an amazing thing happened that shocked all three of us, the beast raised its head and spoke aloud.

"Thank you mighty Princess Yvonne of Angeland, you have spared my life from death, and I am grateful for your help; I shall repay you with my life, because I too want Black and the evil one put to their death as much as you do, and maybe even more-so for what they done to me and my new born." THE Green Dragon smiled and breathed deeply with a sigh of relief as her wounds began to heal and the blood began to stop flowing like water down a mountainside.

"But, but, but that is impossible, beast like you can not speak." Sir Hemsley blurted out in a rude manner.

"Hush my good man, in this world of unbelievable things anything is possible, and it is true from what my dearly departed Mother had told me when I was a child; she said that some dragons and other beast had the gift and power of speech; and yes… indeed it surely is true, they do talk, you did speak to me did you not?" I stood back as the mighty female green dragon arose before us, William and Sir Hemsley quickly leaped backwards out of her way as she flung her mighty tail outward and seemed to wag it as if she were a happy little dog instead of the beast she was. Willy just smiled then he glanced at me with a look of satisfaction because of my deed towards the big ugly green dragon that now stood erect before us and our minds eye.

"Yea My Princess Ich (I) did converse." She bowed her big ugly head towards us and smiled. "Yea, þin bearncennicge (your mother) was a good woman and a tactful as well as a truthful Queen indeed; Ich knew

143

her long ago before she departed to the stars, and hire (her) creator; hēo (she) and Ich (I) talked sometimes when wē were alone in the wilderness where others could not see or hear ūsic (us), we would talk for hours on end about many different things; she and Ich (I)."

The green female dragon fluttered her big hazel eyes and sighed ever so slightly; a tear seemed to flow from one eye as she raised her head and gave a mighty roar that shook the entire cavern, and it echoed throughout as to tell Stella and the Black Dragon that she was not dead after all, but very much alive and ready to fight… longer, harder and stronger than she had ever fought in her life and to bring it on any time they wanted to; that she was ready to fight to the death if deemed necessary in order to rid herself from the menacing harm that they had caused to her after they killed her young one.

"Yea that hēo was; Ich loved my mother so." Ich began to weep a few tear-droplets, but slowly ic whipped them from my eyes, because Ich knew that my royal blood could not allow me to show such things in the presence of my people unless ic wanted to bring shame to my self and my dearly departed parents and other family members.

"Princess, you have the heart of a pure and unselfish Goddess, and Ich know you will be the best ruler and queen that our people has ever had in well over a millennium." Sir William bowed in a dignified and loyal manner as did Sir Hemsley, but the amazing thing on top of it was, that the Green Dragon also bowed before me in loyalty; I could not hardly believe what my eyes were beholding let alone what my imagination was making me think.

"Tis a true statement me Blokes and ye all shall be rewarded once our battle has ended and the Evil Stella and her demon Black Dragon be destroyed. That day, the very day we return to my castle; I promise ye will be Knighted into royalty and you Green Dragon shall be set free to roam as ye may, and I shall dub thee our protector throughout this great land, and this realm we standest in now shall be your domain for all eternity; this I will proclaim and makest into law, and no person shall be allowed to slay thee, this I promise also."

Her words rang loud and strong and echoed throughout the caverns, bouncing off the walls with a clear and precise magical bounce almost as if it came from the pit of bedlam itself.

It echoed deep into the chambers and filtered its way unto the evil Stella's presence, and that bade her mad once she heard the words of her step-sister Yvonne Princess of Davenport and merry 'ol Angeland.

"Black, come here now." Stella shouted. "You have not destroyed the Green one, it is still alive and so is my goody-two shoes step-sister; that meddling so-called self proclaimed Princess… my beautifully ugly step-sister Yvonne and her companions."

Her anger was fierce and it too echoed throughout the cave bouncing about like still another magical ball of hells fire and brimstone; and filtered its way to Yvonne and the others, and as they listened to her words, they began to form a plan to defeat Stella and her evil Black Dragon.

"Prepare thyself for battle Black beast of mine, we shall both destroy those meddlers who dare come into this place, it be mine, tis My Sphere… My Domain… My Realm of myth…and My MIND'S EYE; then we shall go to the Kingdom of my step-sister and her companions, claim it for our common wealth and for all of our eternity to come; this I vow before ye and all darkness; now hear these my words Yvonne, prepare ye thyself for the battle of thy life and prepare ye and your companions to die like the dogs that ye and all art; now; for you Green one; ye shall be in my powers to doest my bidding at my will , doest all ye tyrants hīeran (hear) these My Words, be thee ready my foes, be thee ready… for we come to destroy ye NOW."

Stella's eyes glowed fire red and her minds eye was in a tizzy.

Her words rang loud, and the Black Dragon let out a roar that shook the earth and cave like an earthquake beneath their feet. Rocks tumbled down throughout the terrain like waterfalls flowing at a steady current; after about five moments or so they ceased.

Princess Yvonne and the others were protected beneath the Green Dragons mighty wings; they served them all very well because of their leathery steal like configuration.

"Great Green one, we thank thee for thy protection; art thou hurt in any way my friend." Princess Yvonne poked her head from beneath the mighty wings as the dust cleared the smoldering hot air.

"Aye, (she coughed a couple times) that I am." The green dragon shook its mighty head with fury as the red lava dust flew as if in a whirl-wind.

The smoldering red dust finally cleared the air and settled to the cavern floor; the red powder smoldered beneath their leather sandaled feet and scorched their bottoms to a pitch black with a reddish tent.

"We must leave this cave for fresh air; my mouth is bitterly dry with sulfur; and my chest be a pounding like battle cry drums." Sir Hemsley coughed but did not cover his mouth; and red dust puffed from his parched dry lips with a fury like a mighty dust storm that spewed out of its own cavern.

Yvonne gazed at his mouth as though he had a terrible disease; his lips blistered as if he'd drank hot lava.

Sir Hemsley dropped to the caverns dusty reddened and smoldering floor; he began to blister all over his parchment body as if he had the dreaded Black Death, he began to decay right before the Princess and Sir William's mind's eyes like those who had gone before him, and within moments Sir Hemsley lay dead to the world from which he had come.

The red lava dust was bad enough to the flesh as well as his medical well being; she felt sorry for him, but could do nothing about it until they reached the outside for fresh air and some clean water because the stream in the cave was now hot molten lava, not fit for man, beast nor dragon; they both knew their only hope was the outside world, and not this mystical realm of torment that was brought on by the evil Stella and her wicked demon Black dragon.

Yvonne began to cough as well, and sore spots parched her lips in blistery form also; sort of like canker sores from kissing her betrothed Sir William for hours on end non stop; the pain was unbearable to her as well as Sir William; fresh water would be a thankful and welcome relief to both of them, but first they must reach the outer realm and the river Delta Dawn.

"William my love, we must do all that we can to sooth our parched lips and our lava filled red dusty flesh."

She coughed again several times; her eyes were filled with the still smoldering particles as was Williams.

"Yea my love (chough-cough) that we must (Cough) before we both suffocates right here on this very spot and die; and that I do not wishes upon neither of us my Princess (cough-cough)."

They headed towards the river Delta Dawn as fast as their heavily clothed bodies would allow them to flee the midst from the cavernous demonic dwelling of the evil Stella and her wickedly and most powerful beast... the Black Dragon and all that awful red lava dust that the beast stirred up; almost killing them both.

It would be just the two of them and the Green Dragon against Stella and the demonic Black evil Dragon in the battle of their life here in the pits of bedlam.

Soon they were at the rivers edge, the faint distant roar of the evil one blew past their ears, and they knew that they had time to recuperate before the battle would begin. Taking off all of their clothing they both walked slowly into the cool flowing water and began to wash the filthy volcanic red dust from their nakedness turning the water as red as the ash itself, but is soon settled to the bottom of the river bed allowing them to get cleaner and cleaner.

Their lips began to be soothed as they sipped at the cool flowing water to rinse out their particle filled mouths; they both coughed; hacked and spat red slimy red dust through their gums and over their lips; it burned slightly, but as it began to dissipate their lungs, throat and parched mouth and lips; there was such a soothing sigh of relief to them both as if there was a new beginning on the horizon where a new future looked brighter and brighter as the dawn began to show itself to their now clear bloodshot and reddened eyes.

They walked towards each other and embraced their naked bodies as tight as they could together like a newly formed bond between new laid bricks and pitch on a new home; William began to grow, and Yvonne pushed him back gently, but far enough to let him know that now wasn't the time to make love.

"My Dear William, we must hold our feelings for now my love, their will be plenty of time for our stimulus activities when the battle against my evil step-sister and the evil Black Dragon is completed; know that my love for you will never die and neither shall we; for we will be victorious this day and our people and kingdom will be saved from the longevity of Stella's evil and the black ones menacing destruction; their day is numbered and will be ended in no time." She took a deep breath of a sigh and gave a small unwelcome grin of discontent.

She pressed her naked body tight against his just for a couple seconds and long enough to arouse his interest provoking his enthusiasm and excitement even more, but he knew there would be great love making back at the castle Davenport once they completed their mission and the quest to end all evil for all time to come.

Her voice was calm like the stillness of the woods, not a bird was in the trees, not a creature was pouncing through its harshness; nor were any filtering through the rocks and their crevices.

"Yes my sweet Princess Yvonne, we shall complete this battle fast so we can get back to the castle Davenport where we will continue that which we both need and want to continue, our life together as one in total unity." He smiled at his betroth Princess Yvonne and walked from the stream, dried himself off handing Yvonne her clothes to do the same and they both dressed as fast as they could once the dust from their clothing was shaken off to be as clean as they could possibly be.

"Now we must find some nourishing food, my belly aches from sheer hunger." Yvonne smiled at William and him at her, they kissed passionately for a couple minutes despite the pain in their lips from the blisters, it felt so good to inward spirits that nothing else mattered for that brief time.

"Aye, my love the berries and nuts are ready to be plucked for our needs of hunger; we have time, to replenish our bellies angry roar of hunger."

They both went into the forbidden forest, the trees were still in a calm state of total silence, the bushes blossomed as did Yvonne's bōsm bouncing up and down as if saying I am ready to be taken by thy mouth Sir William, come and get thy milk.

They ate till they couldn't eat another nut or berry, their lips were covered on shades of bluish-reds, and berry blacks, and as they looked at each other, they began to laugh at the colors on their lips and chins.

"Yvonne comest here my love lets me clean thy mouth for thee." He began to lick her lips with his tongue and that sort of tickled her and she began to giggle like a little child.

"William, you make me so very happy my love, but now we must do what we came to do for this past several weeks… kill Stella and that evil Black demon Dragon." She held his hands clasp tight in both of hers as they walked slowly back to the clearing beneath the Black Forest, and as they hammed it up with laughter and jokes, they both knew the seriousness of what was to take place and the harshness of it all may claim both of their lives if they weren't diligent and serious enough for the task they must accomplish together as a united and strong force that couldn't be reckoned with in any such terms of delicacy.

The Sabbath of Witch Stella Her Last Days in the Kingdom of Angeland fast approached and Princess Yvonne and her mighty warrior William prepared themselves in mind; spirit, soul and body in case they would end up being the winner or looser of the battle royal of all battle royals just beyond the sunrise.

As they traveled out of the darkness of the Black Forest they found themselves coming upon a sleepy little hamlet of a meadow; it was none like they had ever seen before. The fortress of the hill lay just beyond the meadow several hundred yards and began to show its own shadow as the sun began to rise higher in the half misty morning sky.

Were it not for the battle between Stella and the Ogre clan several years back the mighty structure where the clan worshiped would remain unremarkably intact as an elegantly constructed Citadel building if it were not for the remains of the jagged rocks, one would swear that it be nothing g more than mere jagged rocks and not a once beautiful Citadel fortress abbey where the clan of Ogre worshiped and dwell, but Stella and her evil demonic Black Dragon saw to it that not only the Ogre's dwelling place, but their very existences would depend on her and not their own way of life as it once was.

Stella had cast an evil spell upon the Ogre clan to make them mean and evil like she and the Black demon Dragon were and that they would do her bidding of evil instead of good like they once done before she took control of their very way of life as they use to have.

There is an air of its connection to the mysteries about the mountainous terrain of the presence of a dozen or so tumulus mounds that surround the fortress; it's almost the focal point of the scenery so to speak like a wise man of old.

Now as it turns out; the Ogre clan and the Village People were once ally joined in an association with another for a common purpose of protection against foreign enemy invaders, but that was soon spoiled by an evil clan of Ogre and their ally to the south where the snow people of Mt Kilimanjaro and Himalayas dwell, they were a nomadic tribe associated with Genghis Khan his band of marauding medieval Mongol and Turkish rulers that once tried to rule the world and still carry the title of respect taken by some dignitaries.

Although academic debate amongst the village people of Davenport Angeland and the Ogre still rages about the origins of the tumulus mounds; from the Medieval rabbit huts to the Castle Davenport to the shambled worship temple of the Ogre and warrants to who or what made the mounds uniquely placed atop the mountains that o'er look the hills and valleys far below its dominion where the border of Ireland and Angeland meet, and as it is said; they have a very powerful and distinct story attached to them.

"There be a saber-edged hillside near by where we can lay wait my lady." William whispered in Yvonne's pointy little ears with a slight trembling in his tone of voice.

"Aye my dear William, I hearest a saber-rattling aggressive threat approaching, with the sundering of a mighty military force." Her tone was mellow and yet on the inside of it was a trembling as well.

As the wind stood still amongst the razor sharp rocks of the jagged hillside, a slight breeze tossed itself above their heads; they both tried to hide themselves like a couple of chameleon lizard slithering be twitched the sharp protruding stones as if they were their own self-made military weapons; and as they both glanced upward with their glitter filled eyes they saw dark shadow of a beasts wings approaching their fortress near a towering razor sharp jagged hillside; they readied their swards for battle; but as they took a closer look at the beast it was only the Green Dragon which had came to help in the battle.

"Princess Yvonne" The mighty Green Dragon shouted with a roar that almost shattered Princess Yvonne's pointy ears as well as Sir William's normal ear... for I must tell you at this time that the beautiful Princess Yvonne was a real Fairy Witch and not a real Human Witch so to speak of. "It be me your protector the Green One; doest thou wishes to make harm of me my Princess." She said with a more mellow tone of voice.

"Thank the God in heaven above us that it is you my friend; I think it be the demon Black one, I do not wish to make harm of you; it is good that you show up now for we prepare for the Battle of Bedlam against my evil step-sister and her demonic Black one; come down here now and wait with us to make surprise attack against our foes."

Aye my Princess, and I too have a surprise for thee as well; do not be alarmed, not in shock, for look behind ye, I bringest ally to help do battle against the evil ones."

"OGRE, WHAT BE THIS; TRETCHERY?" She shouted at them all with a fury of hell fire in her voice.

"No, I convinced the Ogre clan to ally with us to do battle, for they were wronged as well by the evil one; your Step-Sister the evil Stella; she cast an evil spell upon this band of good Ogre to do her evil deeds, but they too wish freedom from her evil powers; they made promise they will do no harm to either of you, and once the evil be destroyed so will their spell be broken and peace will be restored to this their home land once again, for they were once your families ally many year ago, and wish to be your security force as they were your father and mothers security force of long past."

The green Dragon said with a stern tone, even if it were directed towards his Princess the good Witch of Angeland the beautiful Princess Yvonne whom would soon be wed to Sir William Swordspoint...

"May the almighty God in the heavens above us grant us the strength to end my evil step-sister Stella's rain that she has held over our heads for all these many years; I pray Ogre that you and your band of monsters will not turn thy backs upon us; for if thee do, then may the great spirit God destroy you all with his mighty powers, for his are more great than all of us witches in all of the world… so it is said and so it shall be done if you and your band make waste of Sir William Swordspoint and myself… your Princess; Yvonne of Davenport Angeland and the world about us all; I your Princess shall kill you all myself… Is there a clear understanding to this matter thou oh mighty Ogre clan?

"I shall try this spell upon my evil step-sister Stella one more tyme my dear friends; and I pray to all mighty God who has all powers of this realm; our world and the entire universe of Heaven above us all; I pray to he above that this worketh to make the task of destroying the evil black dragon once and for all." Yvonne put here head down, raised both of her now tan arms towards the dark silkweed cave ceiling took a deep breath and moaned like a banshee.

"Ogre takes these items from my pouch and place then before ye and do not ask why."

The Ogre done as he was instructed; but, with bewilderment upon his wrinkled frog butt face.

Yvonne began to chant her spell and turned 3 times to the winds of the cave walls. Her breasts seemed to grow larger at each word as if she were consuming her evil step-sister into her own body; to those who looked upon her made their heads tilt to one side on awe.

Make a Witch as Pure as a White Unicorn

"To make a witch as pure as a white unicorn, you first need the following ingredients…

One sachet of a Unicorn' horn of dust as white as the snows of a winter's mountain top.

One sachet of rose incense

One sachet of white cane sugar

One sachet of finely cut magic herbs selected for their specific spiritual powers.

Three stems from three pure white lilies.

Take the sachet of incense and heat it up with some rose colored incense and a little sugar for a bitter sweet potion.

Next add a small portion of the cut magic herbs for spiritual powers, and stir with the three pure white lily stems and say these words.

𝒫urity, filled with sweetness and spiritual bliss, Angel dust falleth wence this witch drinks this potion fills her with the purity of the white unicorn and give her the kiss of happiness to make her kind and gentle.

𝒯he witch whom this potion is to be given to must drink this in your presence, she friend or foe; it does not matter, it has to be drank in your presence, and you must drink some of the same, but it will not harm nor change you in any way, shape, or form."

"It is done; but I put a slight twist in this spell." Princess Yvonne smiled at the Ogre with a wicked sort of smile that made him blush.

"My lady; what manner of magic be this; white manna falling from the sky; might it be ash from the volcano to the north of here? I am perplexed, and mystified!!! Tell me Princess Yvonne are we doomed to die on this mountain and beneath this white matter?"

"No Ogre and my dear wonderfully brave love William; no we are not doomed, for this is just what we need to help us." Yvonne was cut short by the lead Ogre.

"Yea, yea, snow, snow… how I have longed for this to finally come."

"Ogre, you should not interrupt when I am talking; but thank you for your excited input my new friend; no we shall not perish here for this be manna from heaven, it is Angel dust, that will help the purity spell I have made here before thy feet; here take this and slither thyself to the stairway and place it on the bottom step so my evil step sister will see it when she makes her way to this part of the cave to battle us; I am certain the pleasant odor will entice her senses enough so she will drink it down, and make her evil into purity likened to an Angel" Ich was subtle and giggled slightly with a vary small smile, but a much needed and welcome smile none-the-less.

"No it is not snow, but Angel dust; I have heard of it, but have never seen it until now; and it is a welcome sight indeed, for I know that dragons do not like it because it is said to extinguish their bellies fire." She laughed louder as the dust fell harder and it began to get cold. None of them were dressed for this in climate and sudden weather which she and William had not seen the likes of before until now.

"Snow… snow…snow." One other Ogre yelled out.

"Snow." another shouted right after his brother, or was it his sister? They both jumped like frogs and rolled on the ground with glee and it covered their matted fury hair and froze to it like ice sickles dangling from a tall frozen barn.

Yvonne just couldn't tell unless she had a mighty close look be twitched their legs as to what gender these creatures were; which she did not wish to see now or ever, because of it's ugliness that she'd heard tell of, it was said to look like big cow pies and oblong bull manure and smell just as bad, the thought turned Yvonne's stomach as that thought entered her mind when the two spoke, because their voices sounded like gravel sliding down a mountainside, and sounded like each others voices, no difference between male and female voices so she had heard tell of by her father and mother as a child growing up, but now she knew it was truthfulness that her parents had spoken to her and not fantasy or tall tails like that which she so often is engaged in within this realm of her minds eye.

"Does it hurt Ogre; it looks bad on your barbed wiry hairs." Sir William said with a turned up upper lip and wrinkling brow, he too looked sort of sick to his stomach but just had to laugh so not to think of such foul and unwanted thoughts.

"It does not hurt near as much as whence me sister here pluck em out wit her teeth." He laughed as the other Ogre knelt down and began to do her family Ogre duty.

"Yuck, this is disgusting indeed; me thinks me wilt vomit." William covered his mouth and turned away as the two Ogres one after the other bit into the frozen haze be twitched each others legs and pulled the circle ice away from each others groin area.

"An Ogre must do what an Ogre does best to survive the cold; we must hold our stomachs' so we will be fit for battle if this spell does not work on Stella." Yvonne turned away as well in discuss while the enjoyed the pleasures of the moment.

Soon they were finished their nasty deeds; both had big smiles on their faces from the sheer pleasure they had savored from one another.

"Now we are ready for all battles of bedlam." The female said with a slightly higher pitch to her voice because of all her chewing and sucking on the ice cycles shed plucked from between her brother's legs.

"Now I can tell you are a female Ogre since your voice (uhhhhhhhhhhmmmmm) has changed slightly; will it remain this way from now on?" Yvonne asks with a sensual curiosity.

"Yes it shall as my brothers will also be a deeper tone as a result of what we have just done to each other; it will be good things that have happen to we both." She blushed as a few facial hairs melted off to reveal a slight feminine feature to her face.

"Quiet; someone approaches us; shhhhhheeeesh." William placed his index finger to his lips and shushed the rest.

The lead Ogre had returned from placing the vial upon the rock stairway with a smile upon his face.

"My friends it is only me; I have return... an the evil one drunk the potion as ye say she would; then she choke some and go back up her stair da way she come; she seem to be sing a cheerful song; but me think it might be trick; me no know for sure." He seemed puzzled because his face was all cracked just like a puzzle and ready to be placed back in its box in pieces.

"This might have worked on her; so let us pray that it has." Princess Yvonne laughed and giggled like a little ticklish school girl, her voice hit pitches that would make a dog howl like a wounded wolf.

"Yes; let us pray to our new God in the sky my love, and ask him for his forgiveness for all of our wickedness and transgressions." Sir William looked relieved, his jaw relaxed as if he were asleep in a cozy bed back in the castle Davenport alongside his betrothed to be; the beautiful Princess Yvonne.

The atmosphere seemed tranquil like a trickling stream on a cool summer eve; the must from the cave also calmed itself to a rosy aerosol fragrance, and the temperature started to rise back to a somewhat normality as far as caves temperatures' go.

As Sir William and Princess Yvonne looked at their new friends the huge and somewhat hideous Ogre clan; they looked stunned as the Ogre's slowly began to change their appearances to looking more and more like normal human beings instead of hideous creatures of mass destruction and terror.

"William; is this normal for an Ogre to change their appearances in such an odd manner." She was stunned as she watched the female transform before her bright eyes.

The lead Ogre her brother also started to transform into a human man, but a much uglier sort of species with gray hair like an old gray wolf right out of the prehistoric cave dwellers era.

"My dear friends we have achieved much this day and our victory is almost at hand; but now we must defeat that mean old demonic black dragon of my one time evil step-sister Stella whom; thank God Almighty has now become pure and no longer the evil witch she once was." Yvonne smiled as if there was no tomorrow and began to laugh louder than she'd ever laughed before in her entire life.

"It is one thing to say what a person does as apposed to how they do things and this day, it shall be told like it is without any misconceptions; and you know its almost like painting a picture but with words instead of a horse hair bristle brush and some powdery blood and clay like substance that I shall call paint." The female Ogre said with a gleeful spatter and sputter of her newly formed words that she'd acquired after her transformation from Ogre into a beautiful Human female creature.

"Why Ogre…'err my dear lady, the change is quite stunning to the naked eyes as is your nakedness, here my lady ye must take this my cloak to cover thyself with, said her now human brother as they looked at each other in amazement in as much as they couldn't believe their own mind's eyes, at this rarity of a fantasy known as black hoodoo magick.

Thank thee my… uhmmmm this is sort of a reddish amber moment now isn't it'"

The tall lady Human Ogre exclaimed with her bright fiery red glow upon her freckled cheeks that sort of blended in as if it were icing on a birthday cake made of molten lava and reddish soot from the volcano beneath their feet.

"Bravo dear lady; but we must know your name as well as your brother's name, now that we can have a clearer understanding of your language; ogre was a tidy bit hard to understand if I may take the liberty to say so now that you are … should we say liken to us humans now." Said Sir William with a red glow upon his cheeks as well.

"William, it is alright my brave knight in ragged armor and my husband soon to be; you have seen a new mountain of flesh form right before thy own eyes; and I shall not hold it against thee under these circumstances."

"Thank thee my lady Yvonne; it did play upon my mind's eye as to my view of the big lady's southern exposure so to speak in a frank and awkward manner out of the blue and cool of the cave in which we now stand in awaiting the demon Dragon to do battle in bedlam here with at any moment; for I am a-feared it is in approach to this our location; for I feel its thunderous footsteps in a rumble from a near distant cavern."

The Black Dragon pounced harshly through the caverns like a thunderous tremble from the volcano in which they stood in search of its foe. It was furious at loosing its master the evil witch Stella; for you see after Stella was transformed into a good witch; she turned stone ugly like all the evil that she has once possessed; it was as if old age set in faster than one could imagine; and when she seen her reflection in the watery mirror pool atop her mountain home, she tied a rope about her neck as tight as she could; dove into the pool head first and drowned herself because she never did learn how to swim as a child, and when she was beneath the water it covered itself in a die hardened cask of glass just like a real mirror and there is shall be her grave for all eternity in the reflections of a time that shall soon be long past into oblivion never to return to this life again.

"Now Stella is no longer; we shall ban together as one to end the reign of the Black one for all eternity." Yvonne was rigidly stiff with her words as if to say it is almost finished.

Her voice was low and as soft as a meadow beneath the early morning summer sun.

"Prepare for battle my dear blokes." She whispered her demand.

"Ogres; err humans now, you both need some skins to cover thy selves up with before we battle that black fire breathing beast." William blushed as he stares at both of the giant Ogre Humans.

"Where has the other Ogre fled to, is it a mouse instead of a mighty warrior." Yvonne said with rosy red cheeks to the left and right of her cute little smile of humiliation.

"Oh no me lady, he be back sooner than you think he be; he went to get more help from our clan." The lead giant Ogre now human said with shame on his face from being half naked in front of everyone.

"I must make a wall spell to hold off the Black Dragon till your clan arrive to help us do battle here in bedlam, and I pray he bring you both some pelts to hide thy shame and partial bareness; by the way before I make this spell, I need to know both of your names; and tell me now so I can cast my spell" Yvonne demanded as she usually done since she was the Princess and a spoiled brat who had always got her way.

The big lady went first, cutting her brother off before he uttered a sound.

"I be Freckel-ass Krouse, for I have many little brown speckles upon my face and upon my backside as well, so they call me Freckel-ass; and my brother he be called Time-eon Krouse; because he be created before time begun." Her words spit and spattered with Germanic accents because the Ogre hails from far off Germany on the other side of the mountains and Oceans inlets.

"Me wanted say me name woman; why you do this fo me; me can speak fo me self woman; next time you keep lips closed or me spank ye." Time-eon growled like the animal that he once was oh the outside, but even with his new form he didn't pay much attention to now being human; or at least half human and half Ogre.

He almost took his fist and belted his sister, but was stopped short by Princess Yvonne who just wouldn't tolerate such behavior from anyone or anything.

Ogre's were the first inhabitants of earth and dwell amongst the dinosaurs several thousand years prior; and you could say they once ruled over even the fiercest of dinosaurs the T Rex and Stegosaurs as well as the giant Anaconda Snakes that now hide in the swampy marsh lands on the other side of the world and to the Northern most continent as well as to the mighty Amazonian regions to the south.

"Draw a circle for it contains energy and shall create a wall so that it should not be punctured hastily nor unnecessarily." Yvonne begun the conduct the fiery wall of protection circle spell; and as she did, she herself turned into a fiery flame that would burn any ones butt if the flame got that high to do so.

This frightened the others; for none have ever seen such black magick as this from even the wickedest of witches of their days on earth or in the fantasy world of weird, wicked and evil creatures as the likes of those whose tales this be about.

"This spell was a shorter spell, but more powerful than the first, It shall make the beast go away and give more time for the Ogre clan to come back to help us slay the Black Demon Dragon and send it to the pits of Hell whence it came along with its master… my not so dearly step sister Stella whom is now departed from this mind's eye realm." Yvonne lifted the spell like a mighty door opening all by itself, but at a moments notice and one word fro Yvonne it would once again protect them all from any beast; and that made her grin like she just made love to her man Sir William.

Fiery Wall of Protection Two... The Circle Spell

"Circle start thy fire from within and consume my flesh with thy body

Protect with thy wall of flame and bind us here within thy circle where a demon shall not enter

Candle burn evil when it dray neigh to keep hastily it away

Powder turn to stone; and, make into a vanishing dome before all evil to protect those here which seek thy safety within; now let thy mighty power begin."

As soon as the last word was said, the Black Dragon approached the cavern where Yvonne and her friends were standing. They could see the mighty beast, but it could not see them; and when the beast come near to take a sniff of the mythical dome; its magical flame burnt its big ugly black nose.

"Yeah, this wilt teaches thee a lesson in manners; go ahead and take another snuff; you shall deserve all you get from it." Yvonne was as happy as a Lark in a flowery meadow singing a gleeful song of victory knowing that her spells were the most powerful ones on the entire planet or universe as far as magic spells go out of the mind's eye of witches and those who believe in such things as all of this weird sort of stuff; she was the best of the best.

The mighty black demon Dragon jumped back several feet and shook its mighty head letting out a thunderous roar that shook the cavern; saliva and snot flew from its mouth and smoke filled nostrils from the depths of its fury. He wasn't a bit thrilled from the burn it obtained on its big bumpy black nose that was also covered with many battle scars from Knights trying to slay it, but ended in failure and death for the poor blokes who dare offend its lair, and its life.

The outside of the invisible dome was covered with the slimy muck and the dragon bent down as if it wanted to sniff it again and it even tried to see what was beneath it, but backed off at the thought of getting its nose burnt once again. He shook his head a second time; turned himself about face and blew a big stinky puff of gas out its mighty butt as it walked back to the cavern from whence it came.

About a half hour later the other six from the last remaining Ogre clan on earth returned to the cave; out of breath but stronger than they ever were, I guess its because they ran all the way back instead of their usual slow walking that they were so much of their habitual mannerism.. An Ogre just don't run for any reason and when they do; well it has to be a dang good one.

"We bring pelts for me brotha an sista; them embarrass me an me other brotha an sistas an this no good for they now ugly like most human be; jest no good at all." Bigtoe Klause the muscular Ogre said with his grumpy and rogue gravely voice; but gave a slight funny grin as he looked at his half Ogre and half Human brother and sister with shame. "Here; take… put on so to prepare fo battle with yon black demon beast." he smiles once again because he liked to fight for no particular reason whatsoever; just fight that's all.

Princess Yvonne went doesil (turned clockwise) three times in a state of trance inside the circle and was about to place the purity spell upon the rest of the Ogre so they could turn to humans as well; but she stopped to gather her thoughts instead of continuing.

"Wait a moment I must not do this spell right now; Ogre clan go now and destroy the black demon, that foul smelling beast… the Black Dragon; it must be slain without hesitation… go and do it quickly so we can all go home and be happy finally… and when it is finished we must give thanks to God above who is the creator of us all; GO." She commanded with a power bound tone that echoed throughout the cave and it was like a mighty thunderous howl of a she wolf in heat calling to its mate.

The Ogre's all bowed in respect of her mighty power and being the Princess and soon to be queen of all Angeland and the world beyond.

Once the Ogre clan left the cavern and arrived in the main cave area where the Black Dragon was licking its wounded nose from the sting of the good witches magick; they were surprised by the Green Dragon as well who had come to join them in their battle against the evil one, but they had no real idea and began to not want to fight the now two dragons instead of only one which they were prepared for once they excepted Yvonne's commands just moments ago.

The Green Dragon blew its mighty fire upon the Black one and it jumped high enough to cause a small earthquake that startled the Ogre clan; they looked at each other in bewilderment as to one dragon going against the other; they had never seen such a thing happen before in their realm of uncertainty and fraction of their own mind's eye of common sense to which most Ogre just cant reason or recon with at a moments notice as to their own mighty abilities that they would come to quickly use as well upon the old mean black beast that has so long been creating havoc upon their own kingdom as well as to the kingdom of humans in the valleys below their mountains; once they came to their senses that is.

Now Ogre tend to just do things in a spontaneous methodology; especially in their line of attack towards their foes; but this new ingredient startled them to rethink just a bit; after which the battle of Bedlam was on.

From the moment they left their attack place to join the Green Dragon; the blood and barbed wire hairs flew in all directions. They were scorched from head to toe; from front to back side and top to bottom.

Many an Ogre as well as many a human had lost their lives in fights such as this one, but this time things were different; there were many against one and the forces were with then all more-so because of Yvonne's good black magick she placed upon them to help give then an extra element of power and strength.

Bigtoe Klause took a swipe and trapped his club on one of the beasts spikes behind its ear; but he hung onto his club in spite of the beast flinging him from side to side; slamming him into the caves walls one after the other; in abut 10 minutes of this brutal pounding, the club and Bigtoe flew away from the fury and landed on his head against some razor sharp-jagged edge conical pillars rising from cave floor; these limestone caves can take their toll on any flesh, human Ogre or beast because the stalactites that is gradually built upward from the floor as a deposit from ground water seeping through and dripping from the cave's roof are like spear tips in many different scales in height and circumferences and when one lands on them; they can cause significant damage or even an end to ones mortal life. In the process several of the ceilings stalactites were shook loose and plundered down upon Bigtoe's side and left leg. He let out an awful yell that sent shockwaves abounding throughout the caverns of the cave and in seconds it reached the others ears.

Freckel-ass and Timeeon wanted to leave Yvonne and William to go help their brother and sisters in the fight against the demon dragon, but when they looked at their new human statures, they only hung their head down in a bit of disgust and mortal shame and there was nothing they could do because they were now frail humans; they were both horrified and mortified at the very thought that they might loose still another family member of their clan, of which was the last of their kind on earth.

Freckle-ass began to weep allowing several tears flow down her black cheeks; this was something no Ogre had ever experienced before and all she could think of is that she wished she was an Ogre once again just for a short time in order to be able to help our loved ones out for the last time and still keep the little dignity that she had left.

Timeeon flung his arms around his sister to comfort her but she pushed his arm away; this too was something that an Ogre had never done before in their life, these new feelings were almost as bad as the brutality that the rest were suffering at the battle of the beasts in the pit of Hells fire and the bedlam world of insanity and none-existent fictions reality brought on by some unforeseen mind's eye imagination.

As the battle rages, the Ogre clan was being beat up something fierce; the cavern walls were splattered with blood and wild hair from both Ogre and Dragon and it seemed to be making wild and weird cave paintings of the battle in the process that would soon end in defeat of the Black Dragon once and for all.

One of the paintings was an imprint of Bigtoe being stuck to the powerful beast from his war club; and another showed one of his sisters spread eagle on the floor as if she were drawn and quartered as if her arms and legs were torn from her body like a rag doll that had been divide into four parts by a group of kids that all wanted to own the very same stuffed toy doll; blood dripped from each limb as well as the body, her eyes were plucked out of their sockets and her head split wide open exposing her brains; there was a big gash in her chest that also exposed her still beating heart and when she looked at it while taking a breather behind a large rock, she became faint and passed out on the floor spread eagle and still intact, but with several slash wounds on her arms, legs and across her breast that was partially exposed from her fur top being ripped by the dragons razor sharp claws.

Bigtoe had been knocked unconscious from a powerful blow to his head by the dragon head butting him like a malicious and malevolent wrestler from the WWF of today's sports entertainment on TV; but back in these days there was no such thing as the WWF or TV, just pure and brutal bloody entertainment in the medieval European and old-fashioned style of gladiator and Greco Roman enlightened attitudes of such sports of their days.

Now there were only four doing battle in bedlam and it began to look like both Ogre and human alike was loosing the battle.

In the meanwhile Timeeon and his sister Freckle-ass had snuck away from Yvonne and William when they were busy making out behind some rocks as if it would be their last fling on earth. The two semi-brave half Ogre-half Human brother and sister act were curious about all the screaming they'd heard earlier when the battle first began; they grabbed their clubs and prepared themselves as well for battle. By the time they arrived only two of their kin were left wearily laboring away in mêlée crusade; it was a seemingly endless concerted effort on their ongoing participation in the skirmish at hand.

When they saw the battle was being lost they plunged head-long into the conflict, pounding away left and right at what could be as if lightening were striking from all sides all at the very same instance. Freckle-ass also stolen Sir William's sword and began to slash at the beast's throat as hard as she possibly could; blood gushed out like a Texas oil well and splashed in all directions as the beast flung its head round and round like a merry-go-round… up and down; round and round the two sang in unity causing the dragon to began to feel an atmosphere of being faint and queasy in its big fat belly; all of a sudden it let loose with a mighty spew of bloody and bony slime like vial; its eyes bulged into a protuberance that extended its blackness dangling down from their soft palate core as if they were on a springy body part from a Halloween costume of a zombie.

Freckle-ass and Timeeon stood back and watched as the dragon fought for its last breath of air; a small puff of flame spat out in a last effort to destroy its enemies, but alas it gave up its horrid reign of terror.

What took the others hours not to achieve, the two newly formed humans had accomplished in about fifteen or so minutes; but it was also the rest of the battle that had taken its toll more or less on the demonic Black Dragon. The battle for bedlam was finally over and as soon as it was, those who had fainted awoke in amazement to the feat of their brother and sister slaying their fee fi fo fum of a dumb-dumb beast who could have helped rule the world if its master Stella has survived her demise; but it was not to be; and, the mighty Black Dragon lay dead at Freckle-ass feet; and with a mighty swish from the sward three times on the throat of the dragon, she cut its head off and kicked it aside to rot in its own pit of Hell fire and brimstone for all eternity.

Arm in arm the Ogre clan; bloody as they all were, limped back to the cavern where Princess Yvonne and Sir William were sitting to see and to hear the tale of their confrontational as well as the stimulating conquest of war against pure evil.

"It is finished my Princess" Freckel-ass said as she bowed to her Royal Highness Yvonne and the mighty Knight Sir William, and then continued… "Thank God you have defeated the enemy and you all shall be rewarded greatly; just say thy wish and it shall be yours my dear friends." The mighty she-male Ogre thing-a-ma-bob said as she bowed in respect to unadulterated and complete Fairy Royalty, well at least Yvonne was, but

Sir William… well, he was half human anyway, but none-the-less a Royal pain in the butt as well.

Yvonne was sincere and truthful in her words as she gave them back in favor of a bow of respect and a job well done in their part of the battle for bedlam amongst all her wayward evil bloke in her beloved Angeland.

"My beloved Ogre friend's it shall be peace throughout all the land's to inter mingle as ye please, and this mountain shalt be yours for ever more in this land of enchantment where this Royal Fairy rule till the cows come home and jump over the moon." Yvonne shook their clammy hands with a humble and grateful heart, and then sprinkled Fairies Dust over them; and, they began to change into giant humans and never more would Ogre exist to do harm to both Fairy and human kind alike as time had to change for the better. They all took the oath and made a vow to become Christians and learn the ways of the ancient ones who came before them to a wonderland like none other they had ever seen.

Yvonne stood before the clan and raised her arms beginning her chant to perform the purity spell like she done to help change Timeeon and Freckel-ass to humans and kill her evil Step-Sister Stella the Black witch of the North.

When it was all said and done; not effecting Timmeon and Freckel-ass in any way… just the rest of the Ogre clan, they too were transforming in to humans like they were, and it was all good. The clan now had a new life of freedom and could finally build their own town upon the mountain to live out the rest of their days on if they so desire to do so.

Of course they were all welcome to live back near the Castle Davenport it they choose to, but being their new leader; Freckle-ass wanted them to remain upon the mountain as allies and watchful protectors for all of Angeland and the territories that surrounded them.

"Very well; it shall be as you wish; I shall have the towns people bring you more supplies, and bring you newer building materials and anything you might need to live a good human life as you should have been doing all this while; you will have an abundance of food, and we shall teach you how to cook the proper ways, make clothing and all the rest of the skills that is necessary to live in the human way and not like animals that you once were." Yvonne appointed Freckle-ass Princess of the mountains and the rest Dutch's and Dukes and warrior Knights; she smiled with a joyful smile knowing that her entire kingdom would now be safe from any enemy who dare try to afflict terror upon them. "I shall give Angeland a new name because it is now a peaceful kingdom where no beast will ever dwell ever again; I shall dub this England, because now everyone will speak the queens English as it must be.

"Hail to Queen Yvonne and King William; we are free at last." All the newly formed Ogre Humans cried out in unison and bow down to their new rulers in the land of sheer magic, fantasy, fiction and mystical intrigue.

"This is the time for a triumphant victory celebration; my friends you must come with us back to the Castle, and then you can return to this mountainous home of yours; I must insist." Yvonne now had much respect for the Ogre clan; and it too would be spread like a wild fire throughout the land of enchantment.

"But… but my queen." Timeeon tried to spew out his disarray of words and was cut short by William.

"Now- now Timeon, what the Princess; I mean Queen wants she shall get from all subjects, big, small, human or Ogre-Human, and yes even the beasts of the wild bow down to her command, and you will be no exception is that understood; you are coming with us… it has been commanded by your Queen and now by me your New King. William Swordspoint." His attitude reflected his pale glowing smirk of a half assed smile.

"Since this be the case, we will all come to join in the festive occasion." Princess of the Mountain… Freckle-ass spat her words in a humble and humiliated manner, but commit tingly approved to the command by the Royal couple.

"YEAH… let da party begin, yump." Blurted out the youngest female Ogre-Human… Yulaglade Klause; as her ecstatic senses grew like a new born babe just crying out from its birth spanking.

'It is settled, we bust head down the mountain to the flowing waterways to clean our battle wounds and refresh ourselves and then head back to Davenport in triumph." Yvonne shouted with an over lay of various singing tones of joy about their success.

The happiness, pride, and feelings of elation came from winning, and being victorious over the evil reign of past terror from Stella and the demonic Black Dragon that had caused much destruction and blasphemous Black Magick both here and abroad over the years, but now it was finished. They all thanked God and transformed the whole continent into a Christian social society for all eternity.

Although time overcome its ills in this realm of uncertainty where the creator and the created shall both triumph the many lengthy tasks of making all of this possible through words of wisdom and disbelief whereby fantasy and fiction have came together as one just to free the authors mind's eye of his wonderment of creative insanity with myth, mayhem, and some mighty yucky thoughts; the creators imagination will continue to flourish and spew out more such tales to you the wonderers of eons of time in your own mind's eye where you and I will always thank God for his merciful gift of life he gave to us all… wisdom and intelligence and courage enough to get through many writers blocks and be victorious throughout life even in…

The End

<><><><><> <><><><><>